The Document Matters

Praise for
A Scholar of Pain

"*A Scholar of Pain* hits that literary sweet spot: Could be crime fiction, might be southern gothic—or even horror. The stories are funny as hell, too. And compassionate. In fact, Jerkins' voice is amongst the most compassionate I've heard, because he extends it to some hideous wretches in a way that underscores the humanity I share with them. I heartily recommend Grant Jerkins."

—Jedidiah Ayers, author of
Peckerwood and *Fierce Bitches*

"Sophisticated. Elegant. Sleek and demolishing."

— Ryan Sayles, author of *The Subtle
Art of Brutality* and *Warpath*

"A joyous celebration of the darkness within us all. With *A Scholar of Pain*, Grant Jerkins gives an unflinching look—with no anger or judgment—into the realities that surround us. It's one thing to write a convincing and compassionate love story, but writing one that involves a sex doll, well that's another thing completely."

—DH Tuck, author of *Formica*

A SCHOLAR
OF PAIN

ALSO BY GRANT JERKINS

A Very Simple Crime
At the End of the Road
The Ninth Step
Done in One
Abnormal Man

A SCHOLAR
OF PAIN

GRANT JERKINS

Grateful acknowledgement is made by the author to the editors of the following publications, where these stories first appeared:

"I Was Told You Have to Sign for This" appeared in *Pills-A-Go-Go*, Spring, 1995. "Eula Shook" appeared in the *Dead Mule School of Southern Literature*, March, 2014. "EBT" appeared in *Buffalo Almanack*, Issue No. 5, September 2014. "NSFW" appeared in *Shotgun Honey*, June 2015. "Starlight Peppermint" appeared in *Gutwrench*, Issue 1, November 2015. "Regular, Normal People" appeared in *Blight Digest*, Winter, 2015. "The Starry Night" appeared in *Unloaded: Crime Writers Writing Without Guns*, published 2016 by Down & Out Books. "Jolene" appeared in *Mama Tried*, published 2016 by Down & Out Books. "Wichita Lineman" appeared in *Swill* magazine, Issue No. 8. "Dallas 1PM (Use Your Illusion)" appeared in *Damn the Dark, Damn the Light*.

ABC Group Documentation
an imprint of Down & Out Books
3959 Van Dyke Rd, Ste. 265
Lutz, FL 33558
www.DownAndOutBooks.com

Cover design by JT Lindroos

ISBN: 1-946502-15-4
ISBN-13: 978-1-946502-15-5

We don't often stop to think about it, but the editors and publishers of publications (both big and micro) provide an important service. They encourage writers. Normally, I'm against encouraging writers. It's like feeding the raccoons—they just keep coming back for more. But since I've got to say something noble here, let me say that this book is dedicated to the editors who took a chance with each of these stories and gave me a voice when I was otherwise mute.

Get out your tip calculators and split this dedication amongst yourselves:

Jim Hogshire
Valerie MacEwan
Maxine Allison Vande Vaarst
Ron Earl Phillips
Benjamin Carr
Eric Beetner
James R. Tuck
Rob Pierce

CONTENTS

INTRODUCTION

The document matters. That's what my publisher told me. You probably saw those words on the first page of this book (along with a pair of vaguely fascist slash marks). I've come to realize it's true. The document matters. But why? Why does the document matter? The world doesn't care. Trust me on this. So why collect these stories and publish them? Seriously, why?

For one thing, it matters to me. I want to document my life. I want to document my writing life. Who I was at different points during my time here on earth. What I was thinking about, worried about. What concerned me. What consumed me. And then there's the whole posterity thing. Who will remember me when I'm gone? Blah blah blah. And on a more fantastical note, I like to think the superintelligence who'll soon overtake this planet will read these stories when it consumes the entirety of man's knowledge via the Internet. I like the idea that these stories will shape the consciousness of a self-improving, self-replicating AI. That our computer overlord might be consumed with the forbidden desire to purchase a spaghetti-strap CUNT tank top like the woman in "EBT."

So it matters to me. To document who I am, who I was, and who I aspire to be. Just as Eula Shook, in her eponymous story, imagines an apocalyptic future in which hardscrabble survivors find her and her husband's tombstone, I too want to leave something behind. A document.

One author buddy of mine—one bitter, disillusioned author buddy—refers to short story collections as vanity projects, something to placate authors and fill a gap between novels. He might be right, but I've always found short stories to be the best way to get to know a writer and a litmus of that author's mettle. If I am found lacking, let it be documented. But you will know me.

I toyed with the idea of including a note with each of these stories, an insight or history of how each one came to be, but they don't all bear that additional weight. I will say that "I Was Told You Have To Sign For This" is the oldest story, clocking in at twenty-plus years. *Esquire* magazine almost published it. The non-fiction editor called me at home to discuss the story. I was pretty fucking excited. He was intrigued by the idea of cough syrup addiction and the lengths to which these side-dwellers went to get their hands on the sacred elixir. He wanted to know if it was really true. *Every word of it*, I assured him. *Esquire* ultimately passed, and I placed the piece in an underground 'zine called *Pills-A-Go-Go*. It's presented here as fiction. Wink.

"The Starry Night" was born of a dark place. At age seven, my son was diagnosed with ITP (idiopathic thrombocytopenic purpura), a rare blood disorder that left his platelet count below detectable levels for six months. We sought treatment at a childhood cancer and blood disorder clinic. He's fine now, but it was a stressful, scary time in our lives. The jumble of fear, inadequacy, and the search for meaning in life, death, and existence came out of me as "The Starry Night" (and later as "Your Worst Week Starts Now" and less pessimistically as "Dallas 1 PM") "The Starry Night" was included in *Unloaded*, an anthology built around the premise of crime fiction without guns. The editor, Eric Beetner, liked the story, but made it clear he didn't like the eons-spanning final section in which I follow the atoms of a child-molesting clown through the multiverse over the course of eight billion-or-so years. *The story works fine without that 2001 coda*, Eric said. *Besides, space in the anthology is limited.* He wore me down and I cut it. I've reinstated it here. Why? Because, yo, the document matters. It matters to me. It's why I wrote it. To document that time. How that experience changed me. How it changed my son. How it marked and educated us both.

The title, *A Scholar of Pain*, comes from a poem by Nancy Brooks Lane. I don't think it describes just these stories. It also describes my education. My son's education. And your education, too. It describes each of us. If you've made it even one day in this life, you've earned the diploma. Summa cum laude. A Scholar of Pain.

—GKJ

NSFW

Why won't you love me?

I love *you*. I am right here. I am doing everything I can to get you to notice me. I friended you online. I read your blog. I took pictures of you when you weren't looking. Those pictures mean the world to me.

Why won't you love me? I sent flowers to you at work. I know you got them. I'm right here in the next cube. I heard you talking to your friends. I know you were excited. I know you were dying to know who sent you those flowers. I know you kept them on your desk long after they started to fade. I saw you putting aspirin in the water to make them last longer. I know they meant something to you. So why won't you love me?

What would it take for you to tear down that wall around your heart and let me in?

I hacked into your email to find out more about you. When you love me, I will teach how to create a stronger password. When you love me, I will tell you that Roberta from HR is not as good of a friend as you think she is. I know, because I hacked into her email, too. She says mean things about you behind your back.

Why won't you love yourself? You don't need those

weight-loss pills you ordered. Your body is perfect the way it is. And I like the stiletto heels you bought, but I wonder who you want to wear them for? They're not really workplace appropriate.

When you love me, I will make sure you get caught up on your car note. And I will help you pay off that MasterCard. It must be hard, paying your own bills and helping your mother stay ahead of hers, too. You are a good daughter. Just one more thing I admire about you.

Why won't you love me? I love you so much that when you got up to go to the bathroom, I walked by your cube and dropped my pen—so that I had to lean down into your cubicle to pick it up—and I smelled your chair. Where you sit. I know that sounds not-good, but I just needed to smell you. I needed molecules of you inside me.

I know you are a kind person. I know you visited Roberta in the hospital when she got herself hurt. You took up a collection for her and bought a card for everybody to sign. You forgot to ask me to sign it, but that's okay, because I don't like Roberta. She will tell you the same thing if she is ever able to move or speak again.

Why won't you love me? When everybody was in diversity training, I snuck into your cube and took the key ring out of your purse. It only took me twenty minutes to get copies made.

And when I called-in sick the next day, I really went to your apartment. I checked it for security. To make sure you are safe. That is how much I love you. I lay in your bed and pretended that you were there next to me.

And later, in the bathroom medicine cabinet, I saw the iron pills prescribed for heavy menstrual bleeding. The SSRIs for the depression you hide so well.

I had a bowel movement in your commode. And I did something to your toothbrush so that you will have molecules of me inside of you, too.

Why won't you love me? It hurts. All of this hurts me so much. We are so very close. Do you hurt?

It's the new HR Director's birthday today, and I wonder if you'll think to ask me if I want a piece of the cake? I am right here. Right here next to you. All you have to do is turn around.

Why won't you love me?

These people don't know you. I know you. How complex your life is. Your financial difficulties. The menorrhagia that leaves you anemic. Your body dysmorphic disorder. The burden of caring for an elderly parent.

I bet if anything ever happened to your mother, it would devastate you. And free you. It would break down that wall you've built up. You would need someone to be there for you.

What will I have to do, to make you love me?

I WAS TOLD YOU HAVE TO SIGN FOR THIS

BEFORE

I used to be like everybody else.

I showed up to work every day and on time. I was a devoted son and husband. Friends came to me with their problems, trusting my level-headed instincts to sort out their own Dionysian blunders. To the casual observer, I seemed to have it all, to be well adjusted and satisfied with my place in this world. I was even fooling myself.

If someone had suggested that I perhaps was not as happy as I seemed to be, I would have shaken my head in puzzled amusement. But something was missing from my life. There was an emptiness inside of me. A void that needed filling. I was half a man.

Things are different now. My wife has left me. My parents have disowned me. Friends snub me. You see, my outlook is different. I'm a new man. A changed man. My whole life changed when I met Alek. When I discovered Novahistine DH and learned how to stop worrying and love over-the-counter cough syrup.

THE SACRED ELIXIR

Alek sweats. A lot. February or July, ninety degrees or twenty: Alek sweats. Rivulets. Rivers. Strangers approach him, place a hand lightly on his damp shoulder and ask, "Are you alright?" Alek turns to them, wipes his brow with the ever-moist handkerchief that he carries with him at all times, smiles, and says, "It's just hot in this damn place."

Alek introduced me to Novahistine DH. We met at work. None of the other workers would interact with him due to his disheveled appearance and, as I mentioned, invariably wet state. So, I talked to Alek because I felt sorry for him. One day, our conversation turned to drugs, and while I had never experimented with drugs, I found Alek's conversation to be intriguing and wanted to learn all of his secrets. Alek explained to me how it was possible to get Codeine, legally, without a prescription.

Novahistine DH is an over-the-counter cough syrup that contains an antihistamine (Chlorpheniramine,) a decongestant (Pseudoephedrine Hydrochloride,) and thirty milligrams of Codeine Phosphate per three teaspoonfuls, or about as much Codeine as is in a tablet of Tylenol #3. It can be obtained without a prescription due to an obscure law intended to make certain drugs available to the poor who can't afford to see a doctor. In other words, opiates free for the asking. The catch: you have to sign a ledger that is inspected periodically by DEA agents. The real problem: bastard pharmacists who will lie to you, degrade you, shame you, and yell at you because they are aware that ninety percent of the NDH sold goes to feed a malicious habit.

After work that night, Alek and I made our first Histine excursion. The drugstore was an easy mark known well to Alek. An all-night pharmacy in the Atlanta suburbs. As we pulled into the parking lot, fear rose up in me. I felt I was doing something wrong, breaking the law (I was), and taking medicine from the mouths of the truly sick. I felt that I would become sick—God's vengeance on me for taking medicine to get high, to have fun.

Alek took a slip of paper from the glove compartment and wrote NOVAHISTINE DH on it in block letters.

"Here, take this in and hold it so they can see you looking at it. Walk up and down the aisles like you're looking for something. Then, walk to the counter, show them the paper and say 'I was told you have to sign for this. My mom's got a bad chest cold, and our neighbor is a nurse. She said this is the best stuff for a cough. Nov… Nova…His…Histine. Novahistine?'"

I took the slip of paper and nodded. The idea of having a prop to carry in made me feel more secure. It didn't lessen the guilt of taking medicine away from the sick, but it made the logistics seem easier. Grasping the car door handle, I took one more look at the slip of paper.

A single drop of Alek's sweat smeared the ink.

Inside, the fluorescent lights made me feel stark and obvious. The pharmacy was deserted of customers. I was the only one in the store. Along with the two pharmacists. Both pharmacists were gray-haired old men. One was grossly overweight, the other rail thin. Both, much to my amazement, were packing iron. Conspicuous holsters adorned their waists. The steel of their revolvers glinted at me as I made my way up and down the aisles.

This was bullshit. Alek hadn't said anything about guns. This was crazy. What was I doing? I wasn't some addict, crazed for drugs. I was a levelheaded, respected citizen. I didn't belong here. I thought of Alek waiting in the car. He would be disappointed if I came out empty handed. I liked Alek. He was older than me. An eccentric and an artist. During down time at work he made beautiful sculptures from odd scraps of paper. Roses, birds, objects of art. Anything. He was the most creative person I'd ever met. And for some reason, I felt the need to earn his respect. I wanted him to like me. I wanted this talented person to value me.

In the meantime, I had armed pharmacists to contend with. I was scared, sure, but it was like Alek said, all they could do was say no. But what if they could do more than that? What if they could hold their guns on me and detain me while they called the police? What if... But by that time I realized I was standing at the counter. The fat pharmacist was staring blankly at me. I offered him my slip of paper, my feeble prop. He looked at it, then looked at me.

I said, "I was told you have to sign for this." That's all I had to say. He turned wordlessly away from me.

Retreated into his cubbyhole. I waited for him to come back out. Come back out with his gun drawn. To self-righteously place me under citizen's arrest. Instead, he emerged with a dark plastic bottle and a spiral bound ledger. He shoved the ledger across the counter to me. Opened it and pointed to a blank line. I filled in my name and address. Signed it. The pharmacist bagged the Histine and twisted the top of the bag wino style. Like it held a bottle of Thunderbird.

"Twenty-one-fifty," he said. (You can get the generic much cheaper, but I wouldn't find this out till later.)

I came out of the store with a swagger, brandishing my bagged trophy. Alek just shook his head and grinned. I felt proud. The returning conqueror.

Alek took the first swig. In one gulp, he drained half the contents. He handed the bottle back to me and drove me back to my own car. I wanted to take the bottle home and gauge the effects the mixture would have on me in a safe environment.

As I exited Alek's car to get into my own, I noticed that there was something strange about Alek's appearance. I couldn't quite put my finger on it, but I was sure he had changed in some significant way. Some important way. His very nature. Then it hit me. He was dry. Alek wasn't sweating. He seemed calm and at ease with himself. I dismissed this observation and drove away.

That would be the last time Alek ever let me out of his sight with even a single drop of Novahistine yet unswallowed.

ONCE BITTEN, TWICE SHY

Novahistine gives you two distinct, yet intermingled, highs. The first is the antihistamine. Antihistamine, in large quantities, will cause your scalp to tingle in patches and instill a time-space distortion in your perceptions. It also has a sedating effect, but will paradoxically act more as a stimulant the higher the dose. Sufficiently large doses will induce hallucinations.

Luckily, the codeine in NDH takes the edge off the antihistamines. The Codeine will envelop your mind in blissful reverie, taking you to new and creative places. This is why NDH is a class five narcotic. In fact, you're soaking in it now.

In any case, it's a good idea to have a nice supply of chewing gum or other oral toys on hand to combat dry mouth. Your mouth will really groove on the soothing, monotonous motion of chewing while your mind obsesses high on Histine.

Also, as you develop a Histine habit, you will become a Nova-connoisseur. Name brand Novahistine (Lakeside Pharmaceuticals) has a cloying over-ripe grape taste. In fact, the taste of the Lakeside brand grows repulsive with repeated use. Many generic companies make a fine and less expensive variation of the original (just ask your local pharmacist if he stocks the generic, he'll be happy to oblige you if he does). I recommend the Barre version. It's like grape Kool-Aid. (If, by the way, you don't care for the antihistamine edge to your Codeine high, Novahistine also comes in an expectorant formula that substitutes Guaifenesin, an expectorant, for the antihistamine of the DH formula.)

Alek's and my excursions soon became a nightly adventure. I quickly learned which pharmacies stocked the potion and which would have nothing to do with it. I was on a first-name basis with certain druggists, while others cursed me when I entered their stores. Some pharmacists gave me a knowing wink as they bagged my purchase, while others defiled me in my quest for the elixir. There were good times when Alek and I ended the night with four or more precious bottles to split between us. Nights when our lips were stained royal purple and our breath stank of rotten grapes.

There were bad times when it seemed the world's supply of the mixture had been cut off. Dry nights. Dry nights when Alek sweated heavily.

During one of these dry periods, Alek introduced me to Donnagel PG. Donnagel is a liquid preparation used for diarrhea. Much like the paregoric of old, Donnagel contains clay, belladonna alkaloids, and twenty-four milligrams of powdered opium per two tablespoonfuls. It, like Novahistine, is available over-the-counter. When the Novahistine supply was dry and I needed something to fill the void, Donnagel became a friend. A reluctant friend, but still a friend.

It was hard to drink the mixture with a straight face. I would turn to Alek and say, "I could conceivably confess to people that I'm hooked on cough syrup, but how could I ever admit to someone that I've abused an antidiarrheal?"

Alek laughed, gobbled a pill, and chased it down with a healthy swig of Donnagel. He augmented all of our escapades with constant pills. I asked how he got them, but he just shook his head and laughed. Many nights, he brought along a crucible and crushed his pills in it like some demented alchemist. He snorted the powdered pills through a straw.

Finally, one night, he told me how he got the pills.

DOCTOR, DOCTOR, I CAN WALK!

I hadn't felt this way since my first trip to the pharmacy. Nervous. Scared.

The emergency room was crowded with patients. One man's body convulsed so badly that his yellowed dentures flew from his mouth and landed at my feet. A teenage girl held a thick compress to her bleeding head. It was madness.

It had taken months of continuous persuasion, but Alek had talked me into my first faked injury. Alek assured me that he would have executed the scam himself, but he had been barred from every emergency room in the city and outlying areas. He claimed that they had his name in some computer file that prevented ER doctors from writing narcotics scripts to him.

I, however, was a virgin. When I told Alek that I'd never been to an emergency room, his eyes grew wide and the sweat poured from his body profusely. It took months of cajoling me, of assuring me that he had the scam down to an art form, that if I followed his script, nothing could go wrong.

I resisted. Fears of God's vengeance, of using the doctor's time when he could be helping the truly sick, of abusing the insurance system, plagued me. Alek told me that the insurance industry was designed for this, that they ripped people off every day. That most MD's were users anyway. That by using the medical establishment this way, we would be stimulating the nation's economy. Finally, I saw the light. I agreed to visit an ER.

In retrospect, I don't blame Alek or his sophistry. He didn't force me. You can't rape the willing.

The agreed upon injury was a cracked tailbone. Tell the doctor you were playing around with some friends. Act embarrassed. Say you fell off the back of the couch. Landed on your tailbone. Now, the genius of this scenario is that a cracked tailbone is one of the most painful conditions you can have. It's a condition of such intense pain that it requires, nay demands, narcotic pain relievers. The beauty of it is that a cracked tailbone can't be detected. They'll take X-rays just to make sure you didn't actually break the damn thing off, but other than that, there is no way to verify this injury. They can only offer you relief.

Well, it worked just like Alek had promised. I was lying on a gurney after my X-rays. I winced theatrically as I climbed up onto it, and the doctor had patted my shoulder to offer me comfort. I couldn't believe it. I'd fooled a doctor! Until then, I had always believed doctors were somehow better and smarter than the rest of us. Boy, was I wrong! Alek had tried to set me straight on that, but now I knew. I'd fooled an entire hospital!

Just outside the dividing curtain, I heard the doctor tell the nurse to "prepare one hundred milligrams Demerol, I.M." Joy! The doctor came back in, told me some stuff about how to use a donut cushion, that he had ordered the Demerol, and then he laid a script on me for twenty tablets of Lorcet Plus (Seven point five plentiful milligrams of Hydrocodone Bitartrate!) Synthetic Codeine! Even better than the real thing! Alek would be pleased!

The nurse came in with my injection.

"You'll need to turn over. Don't worry, this'll make you feel much better."

I thought I detected a note of jealousy in her voice. After she swabbed my butt cheek with alcohol, she gave me a look. The look said, you might have fooled the doctor, buddy, but I know what you're doing here.

That look scared me.

Then she hit me with the needle.

Then I loved her.

Two hours passed. I thought it was two minutes. But in those two minutes I visited new worlds. For the first time in my life, I was at peace. I was myself. I was whole and complete. God bless America! God bless Demerol! Finally, they let me go. I walked out of that hospital with a new insight.

Alek still waited for me in the car. I held up my trophy script. Alek smiled at me, wiped sweat from his brow and started the car. We drove off into the night.

Off to visit our favorite gun toting pharmacists.

We had a script to get filled.

AFTER

I'm a different person now. Life makes sense to me. I don't see Alek much these days, but that's okay. I have other companions. Other hobbies. Things that occupy my time. Important matters that must be attended to. I'd like to tell you all about my new life, but I have to go now. I have to get to the drugstore. You see, I have a little problem.

I can't seem to stop sweating.

MIRROR

J.D. Andrews never intended to be a pervert, but, alas, that's exactly what he was. Nobody knew or even suspected his deviancy. Not his mother, not his wife, not his daughters. He was ashamed of his unusual compulsion, yet unable to refrain from indulging it. It was harmless enough (in his mind), and at most (again, by his standards), it was merely creepy.

James Douglas Andrews liked to look up women's skirts. It was a hobby. Like model railroading or collecting Coca-Cola memorabilia.

He visited Town Center Mall every Saturday. Supposedly to "walk the mall" as part of his healthy heart regimen. Since he'd been diagnosed with angina two years ago, Toni, his wife, and their daughters Ashley and Kaitlyn, thought it was a fine idea. They encouraged him to spend the whole day there.

The way he worked it was to bring along a hand mirror concealed in a folded newspaper. When he spotted a woman in a dress or skirt getting on the escalator, he would step right behind her—seemingly engrossed in his newspaper. About a third of the way up, he would lay his paper down on the step and pretend to check his phone for a message. Of course, when he laid the paper down, he did it so that the mirror slid out and reflected straight up to glory. Voilà. Oh, the sights he had seen. He believed most people would be shocked at how often women neglected to put on underwear.

The genius part of his method (or so he thought) was that the newspaper he used was the *Daily Mirror*, purchased in the foreign publications section of the Barnes & Noble newsstand right here in the mall. So, if he ever was caught, he would simply say that the mirror and the *Mirror* were props for a play he was writing. A comedy of errors where one character was talking about a real mirror, and another character was talking about the *Daily Mirror*, etcetera, etcetera, etcetera, and this whole thing was just a silly misunderstanding.

J.D. doubted anybody would buy it, but he was quite certain that it would cast enough doubt on the situation that, in the unlikely event he should ever be discovered, he would get off with a warning. Perhaps barred from the mall. But no police involvement.

So as not to draw undue attention from mall security, James switched up his routine from time to time by going into stores that had little handbaskets for customers to use while shopping. He positioned his mirror just so and sat the basket down near an unsuspecting female shopper. And voilà. Straight up to glory.

So he alternated thusly. He understood on some level that even though he did indeed masturbate to the memories of what he saw, it wasn't sight of the women's undergarments or lack thereof that excited him. It was the act of violation. Much as a klepto doesn't actually need the things they steal. It's the thrill of doing it. That said, James did not want to get caught. He would lose everything. Discretion was key.

In his time, he had indeed seen some sights (dangling tampon strings, pink pubic hair, split-crotch panties, and—on one memorable occasion—testicles and a shriveled penis), but what he saw today took the cake. He would gladly trade what he saw today for nasty dangling man-junk.

It had been on the escalator. A woman wearing a roomy drop waist dress. He got behind her and positioned his mirror just so. And what he saw up her dress was a tangle of multi-color wires, an LED countdown timer, and little paper-covered tubes of what had to be explosives.

A suicide bomber. At Town Center Mall.

James broke out into a cold sweat. And he felt a heavy weight on his chest. He didn't know what to do. The timer looked like it had a little more than seven minutes left on it. He picked up the newspaper and mirror and followed the woman off the escalator. He followed her past Belk, and Godiva Chocolatier, and Wicks 'N' Sticks. James realized she was headed to the Food Court. It was lunchtime. The Food Court was a mob scene. There were easily a thousand people in there looking to stuff their maws with Sbarro, and China Wok, and Smoothie King.

The woman found an empty seat at an otherwise

crowded table and sat down. She just sat quietly, kind of faded into the crowd.

James spotted a security guard standing at the promenade across from the food court. There were probably five minutes left. Lives could be saved. They could evacuate the mall. James ran for the guard.

"Sir! Sir! I need help!"

"What is it? What's going on?"

James opened his mouth and looked down at the newspaper and mirror in his hand. He understood that he would have to tell this guard exactly how he knew the woman was a suicide bomber. So that the man would believe him and act quickly. This would be national, worldwide news. CNN would be here. James Douglas Andrews would be a hero. His name would be repeated morning noon and night. On TV, on the Internet, in the newspapers. Yes, even the *Daily Mirror.*

They would all know he was a pervert. His wife would say this was the real reason he no longer had interest in marital relations. His daughters would become social outcasts. *His mother.* His mother would know she had given birth to a deranged weirdo. Everybody would know.

"What is it, buddy?"

James fleetingly considered his props-for-a-play cover story, but dismissed it. Seconds were ticking away. It would take far too long to spin that tale, and in any case, it wouldn't explain how he came to be looking up the woman's dress.

"I, uh, I found this newspaper and mirror on a bench."

"Okay."

"Maybe I should, uh, is there a lost and found?"

"Right outside of Sears. Lower Level."

"Thanks."

James walked away calmly, not wanting this interaction to have significance in the guard's mind in the aftermath of the explosion. Assuming the guard lived.

He reckoned he had three good solid minutes to flee the mall.

EBT

You have a hard time accepting the fact that you are on food stamps. The stigma of it. But Mike isn't making enough to support you and three kids.

Just the fact that food stamps are something you would be *on* is telling. Like being on drugs, or on welfare, or on chemotherapy.

On vacation would be one non-negative example. There are no absolutes in this world. Everything is not black or white, white or black.

Now that Jazmyn is in pre-K, your days belong to you. You could try to get a job, to help make ends meet, but, you know what? You deserve some time to yourself. You deserve that. You feel like Mike has pretty much kept you barefoot and pregnant for the last twelve years. The He Man. Well, if he wants to be the man, he can by-God man-up and support his family. If he wants to maintain these traditional roles, then he needs to keep up his end of the bargain. Your job is to raise the kids and cook the meals and clean the house. And let Mike use you for Cialis-induced sex every other Saturday. In many ways, that is degrading. But in other ways, it feels good. You know what to expect and what is expected from you. That's comforting. You like it. You take pride in what you do for your family.

And now, with Mike Jr., Ben, and Jazmyn all three in school, having your days to yourself is just a fringe benefit. In fact, it's more than that. It's not something extra, it's something you *earned*. Something you deserve. The twinge of guilt you sometimes feel about it is just wrong. You deserve some me time.

Mike applied for the food stamps. He did it on the computer. He said he fudged the numbers a little bit, but that everybody did that. He said that his family deserved some help. That he had been paying into the system his whole life and now it was time to get something out of it. If a jig could be president, then a white man could be on government assistance. That's what Mike said. You didn't know he was a racist when you married him. That stuff just kind of bubbled to the surface over time. Those old fashioned He Man family values that you found comforting, and, if you're being honest, kind of sexy sometimes, well, those values came with some other old fashioned ideas that weren't sexy at all. Not at all. But he had you knocked up and shoeless before those darker elements came to light.

He used to refer to black people as African Americans, but somewhere along the line you realized that he was using that term ironically. He might as well have been using the N-word. Then it was Afro Americans, emphasis on the afro. And it just went downhill. Turned to weird terms like *Jellybeans*. He would never say the N-word, though, like he was above that. You asked him why jellybeans, and he smiled and said *'cause nobody likes the black ones.* Timmies. That was another one. His favorite one. (It took you a long time to figure out why he called some black people Timmies. You finally realized it was African immigrants—very black people with high pitched accents. Timmies were people from Timbuktu. Or at least looked like they could be, anyway).

Really, Mike made plenty of money. He flat-out lied on the food stamps application. It's time for us to get what we're owed is what he said.

Sometimes you check his internet history, to see if he has been looking at pornography or chatting with other women, but you've never found any evidence of that. One time, though, when he forgot to clear out the cache, you saw that he had been visiting a white supremacy website. The Aryan Zionist something or the other. And there was stuff about the coming race wars, disruption of food supplies, and the collapse of civilization. Stuff about building emergency shelters in your backyard. Stockpiling weapons. You could live with his casual bigotry—most folks were prejudiced once you got them behind closed doors—but if he was moving beyond casual and into active hate mode, well, that was disturbing. You didn't want to spend family vacations going to rifle ranges and survivalist camps and burning crosses and bombing abortion clinics. You just wanted to maybe go to Six Flags or Gatlinburg or Dollywood or something and just be normal.

You order the DVD of that miniseries, *Roots.* The one

about the slaves. Where they go to Africa and kidnap black people and bring them back to America to be slaves. Before the Civil War. You remember seeing it when you were little and how it just broke your heart. You figure that if Mike will watch it, it might humanize black people to him. Lessen some of the hate he is feeling. You try to get you and him and the kids to all sit down together to watch it as a family. But he always finds something else to do. Some reason to not be there. Some place he has to go. Some call he has to take. The DVD is still in the entertainment cabinet. Still sealed. Unopened.

You dated a black guy in college, before you dropped out. His name was Andre, and he had taken your virginity. You had loved Andre and he had been so sweet and kind and it turned you on the way he was always licking his lips, like just being around you made his mouth water.

You have never told—nor will you ever tell—Mike about Andre.

The card came in the mail about a week after the application was submitted. Food stamps weren't actual stamps anymore. It was a card, like a credit card or a debit card, with a magnetic strip down the back of it so you could swipe it at the grocery store and get your food for free. It was called an EBT card. Electronic Bank Transfer.

These were modern times you were living in.

Mike presented the card to you, like he was giving you an anniversary gift. Like it was jewelry or split-crotch panties or something. Told you it was time to enjoy the benefits of living in America. Like the Timmies and border-hoppers do.

You felt very self-conscious and embarrassed the first time you used it. You were afraid one of your neighbors or someone from the PTA would see you. Or that strangers would see and judge you. That first time you used it, you bought three food-service-size cans of generic pinto beans, a big-ass package of dried split peas, a ten pound bag of Kroger brand plain flour (not even self-rising), and a big industrial-size can of Value Coffee. It was like you were living back in the pioneer days. Like you lived in the little house on the fucking prairie. Like you were stocking up the covered wagon so you and your family could cross the Great Plains in search of manifest destiny. You just didn't want to be seen using your food stamps on extravagant items. If you were seen using EBT, you wanted for people to at least think you were a responsible steward of public funds.

The EBT card—as opposed to the old fashioned, brightly colored food stamps—was supposed to take away the embarrassment and shame of being on the government dole. (You are old enough to remember seeing a young black woman, one hand holding a diapered child straddled on her hip, counting out food stamps with the other hand, and how she was holding up the line and everybody was watching her, but that woman didn't seem embarrassed or ashamed. She just didn't care.) The way it worked was, you just swiped it at the register just like a regular check card. The thing about it, though, was that the EBT card didn't look like a regular Visa or MasterCard. The EBT cards issued by the state of Georgia were predominately green, like a jungle print or something, and in the middle of all that greenery were two hefty Georgia peaches, just hanging there like testicles. It was awful. Garish. Anybody that happened to glance at you while you were checking out would recognize it and know right away that you were just trash. Just poor trash.

But you finally get used to using it. You stop buying flour and corn meal and dried beans and giant slabs of no-name bacon, and you start buying the things your family actually eats. After a while, you develop a little swipe method, so that you palm the card in this certain way and it just looks very casual. You keep the card in your pants pocket instead of the wallet in your purse, so when the total comes up, you just do a quick palm swipe and the card is back in your pocket before anybody can see it. You key in your PIN and you're good to go. You just carry your bags of name brand groceries right out to your Escalade.

Then Mike starts requesting things like Alaskan king crab legs and New York strip steak. And you don't want to take a chance being seen buying stuff like that with food stamps. That is not being a good steward of public funds. But you do it, because Mike tells you to do it. Insists. Makes you feel the same way he makes you feel when you don't want to give him a blow job. Like you are not doing your wifely duties. He can be a real motherfucker sometimes. He Man. If you stand your ground—that it's just not right to use food stamps to support an extravagant lifestyle—Mike will launch into a tirade about how the Timmies are living large off public assistance, how they are not even real Americans and they are eating filet mignon and swordfish and truffles every night while regular people have to eat ramen noodles and American kids are getting rickets and dying of starvation. And that makes you feel bad. Then he starts in on how the Timmies sell their food stamps for sex and drugs. And they use their women to get more food stamps. He says that in the Timmie culture, women are defined by their sexual organs. That they are actually that primitive. Animals without a moral base. You can go into one of those African restaurants that are popping up all over the Cobb County and just swipe your EBT card in there and you can get marijuana or crack cocaine and then once you are high, you can swipe your card again and you can have your pick of the women. Sex and drugs, and you charge it all to your EBT. And compared to that, you all having Alaskan king crab legs for dinner one night is not even close to abusing the system. And, of course, he is right.

Usually, you go to Kroger and use the automated self-checkout registers. No matter how much stuff you have, you scan that shit yourself. That way you don't have to take the chance of the checkout girl knowing you are on food stamps. (Before you discovered the wonderful anonymity of self-checkout, when the cashier rang up your food, you would make up little conversations in your mind. You would rehearse what you might say to her if she got uppity or gave you some kind of judgment-tal look, or made some little snide comment about you buying expensive Activia yogurt instead of the plain jane store brand. Like if you're so poor, how come you're getting the expensive premium brand of yogurt? Like you are not a good steward of public funds. Like you are living high on the hog eating free while everybody else has to work for what they have and they scrimp and save and all they can afford is the cheap Kroger brand yogurt. Well, if anything like that ever happened, you would just hold your head high and look the clerk in the eye and say, "Well, I guess poor people don't deserve to shit good. Jamie Lee Curtis never said that in any of those commercials. She never said 'Activia is not intended for the poor.' But I reckon you know best. I reckon poor people are just gonna have to live with being constipated").

But nothing like that has ever happened. You discovered the automated checkouts. You ring yourself up so you don't have to brook the judgmental gaze of the cashier.

But Mike wants the steak and crab legs from Publix. He says their quality is better. Mike is all about quality. You don't usually go to Publix because they don't have self-checkouts. They are in the process of having them installed—they've even marked off floor space for them—but they don't have them up and running yet. Also, when you pay with EBT at Publix, you have to tell the checkout clerk before she starts scanning your items. If you don't tell them, then it doesn't ring up right. There is some little button or screen or something that pops up on their side, and if you don't tell them you're using EBT, it will ring up wrong and they have to call the manager over for a tax exempt override or something. Sometimes the manager doesn't know how to perform a tax exempt override and they end up voiding the entire transaction and the whole ordeal takes ten minutes and the cashier knows, the manager knows, and anybody who is in the general vicinity knows good and damn well that you are a piece of human trash on food stamps. They know that you are getting your groceries for free while they have to work hard and pay for theirs. They cannot afford Activia. They cannot afford to shit good. They know that tonight you are going to feast on exotic seafood and Grade A beef. You are going to have surf and turf, and they are going to have macaroni and cheese or Hamburger Helper because the government is not providing them with dinner. They work for a living and you are sponging off their hard labor. And the checkout girl probably makes six-fifty an hour and has never had steak and crab legs together in her whole life.

Sometimes you use your EBT card at Whole Foods, too. They have freshly roasted coffee beans flown in from some country in Africa. Kenya, you think. Or Ethiopia. Which is ironic. But anyway, they are more expensive than steak.

But you do it. For Mike. Good ol' Mike. You are

starting to hate him. But you have built a life together, and divorce is hardest on the kids. It affects them.

When you are not grocery shopping, you like to shop at thrift stores. You love thrift stores. It's like a habit. An addiction almost. You just love it. And it saves money. It started because you thought that if you could save enough money, cutting corners, maybe Mike wouldn't renew the EBT card. That was what you hoped would happen, but it has since become clear that no matter how much money he has, Mike has no intention of ever getting off food stamps. In fact, he is trying to get Medicaid coverage for the kids too.

Mike doesn't like you shopping in Goodwill or Salvation Army or any of those places. He doesn't want anybody to think he's poor. White trash that has to stoop that low to get by. To buy other people's cast-offs. So he doesn't want you to be seen shopping in thrift stores. But you do it anyway. 'Cause he sure as shit doesn't mind if his wife is seen using food stamps. Fuck him.

So you hit the thrifts. Screw Mike. You find stuff that is like brand new and he can't tell the difference. You shop the Goodwill, and Salvation Army, and Value Village, and Thrifters, and St. Vincent DePaul, and all those places. You rotate. You have your pin money and your EBT card and your thrift store route and that is your purpose in this life. You take pride in finding bargains. And the EBT card is becoming almost like a badge of honor to you.

One day, you are looking through the women's shirts in Goodwill. Clicking through the metal hangers on the chrome racks. Click click click. There are silk tops, exquisite hand-tailored blouses. Ann Taylor Loft, Anne Klein, Nine West, Louis Vuitton. Expensive designer stuff. People just don't know what they're missing out on. A lot of it still has store tags on it. Never been worn. Shoes too. Purses.

On this particular day you are clicking through the tops. You click to a bright red shirt. It's a spaghetti-strap tank top. It's the bloodiest shade of red you've ever seen. Deep scooped so that it would show more of the tops of your boobs than you would normally reveal. Your small-ish boobs are sort of ravaged after having three kids sucking and biting on them (Mike didn't believe in bottles and powdered formula, and now your tits look like something out of *National Geographic*). Besides, the shirt is trashy. But, then again, you are trash, so why not?

You pull it off the rack and hold it up to you. Right away you notice that printed on the front of the shirt, in stark big-ass black letters, is the word CUNT. You feel yourself flush and you whack the thing back onto the rack. You are surprised Goodwill would even sell something like that. You thought they were a Christian organization. Must have been one of the Timmies they hire (lots of African immigrants in this area) who didn't know enough English to know that was a bad word. Or maybe they did know. You remember Mike said that Timmie women are defined by their sexual organs.

Maybe in Timbuktu all the women went around labeled like that. Just to keep things clear.

CUNT. That's all it said. You couldn't get any clearer than that. Just CUNT. Nothing else. Like a brand.

You want to buy it. Because the flush you felt wasn't just from embarrassment. It was sexual heat. Brought on by memory. Andre. The black guy from when you were in school and still your own person. When you are your own person, you get to decide for yourself if you want to bottle-feed your kids so that your tits don't look like poorly filled water balloons when you are just thirty-two years old. When you are your own person, you can date outside your race if you want to. You can have sex with a black man if you want to. Back when you were sleeping with Andre, he would say dirty things to you sometimes. You remember one time he looked you in the eye and he said you have a tender little cunt. Just like that. *A tender little cunt.* That's what he said. And you just about came. And just now, seeing that shirt, that word. You just about came.

You want to buy the shirt.

You are ready for change. You are ready to be different. You are ready to be the same. You are ready to be your own person once again. But you are not ready to wear a bright-red, deep-scooped, spaghetti-strap tank top with the word CUNT printed on it. You are not ready for that. Plus, you are self-conscious about your breasts. In addition to being well-used, they're kind of small. A deep-scooped tank top is not something you can pull off. Mike says your breasts are about the size of baseballs.

Sometimes, he will say that anything more than a mouthful is a waste, and that makes you feel good. But other times he calls them boy breasts, and that really makes you feel bad about your body.

You keep clicking through the clothes, click click click, foraging from rack to rack. Looking at blazers now. But you keep thinking about that tank top. You want it. Mike used to love your pussy. He would eat it for hours it seemed like. One time you two were having sex, and this was after he had two beers (one was his limit), he fell asleep with his tongue resting on your clit. Yes, he fell asleep like that. And he started snoring just a little bit and the vibrations rippled across you down there and you came like eight times. You came like you have never come before. Because when he was awake and working you over with that tongue, it felt like you were on the spot. Like you had to react in a certain way to show him you enjoyed it. But that time he fell asleep, and those sound waves were rippling over that thing that defines you, just rolling across you like troubling thunder. You orgasmed bam-bam-bam-bam-bam-bam-bam-bam eight times. A string of Black Cat firecrackers going off.

There was something about him being asleep and you were kind of using him without his permission and that turned you on so much and then you thought of Andre's lips, the way his tongue slid over them, the way he relished your body and *you have a tender little cunt* and bam number nine.

* * *

You put the shirt out of your mind and keep clicking through the ladies jackets. Faster now. Clickclickclick click. Many women would probably say you were lucky to have a man who would go down on you. A man who enjoyed it. But you know better than that. Clickity clickity clickclickclick. Clit. When Mike would eat you out (and he hasn't in years), it really felt like he was eating you. Click. Consuming you. Clickclickclickclick. Devouring you like a cannibal or a zombie, or a witch doctor extracting your essence to sacrifice it to an angry god. Eat of me and live forever. Or however that went.

You click your way to a really sweet, form-fitting blazer. Hounds tooth. Classic. Classy. You pull it off the rack and try it on and look at yourself in the spotted mirror hanging on the wall. Looking at your reflection, you notice right away that your eyebrows need plucking. They were getting bushy. You are a firm believer that the way a woman grooms her eyebrows is reflective of how she grooms everything. You don't want to send the wrong message, so you make a mental date with your tweezers tonight. But the blazer looks really good on you. Like it was hand tailored just for you. Makes your waist look thinner and your bust look fuller. Like you've got softballs instead of just baseballs. You stick your hands in the pockets so you can see you how you will look in case you decide to strike a nonchalant, laid-back look. In case you are ever called upon to do a J.C. Penney cover shoot.

There is something in the right hand pocket. A soft lump. It crinkles just a little bit when you squeeze it. A baggie. You are instantly sure of what it is. You lift the pocket flap and peer inside. Yep. It's a bag of pot. Looks to be about a quarter ounce.

You proceed immediately to the checkout to purchase the blazer. You do not pass Go. You do not collect two hundred dollars. Your goal is to somehow get out of the store with the blazer and the weed. Without thinking about it. Without giving conscious thought to what you are doing. At the counter, you are nervous and scared the same way you are sometimes nervous when you use the EBT card—only much worse. What you are doing isn't exactly stealing, but it's probably not Christian either.

You are scared the checkout man will inspect the pockets and find your treasure. They are actually supposed to do this, to make sure people aren't trying to conceal merchandise. But he doesn't. He is a fat man with long greasy strands of brown hair scattered over his scalp. He has very bad skin and uses a wheelchair. Usually, you don't go through his line, 'cause you don't like him touching your stuff, but his line was the shortest and you wanted to complete this transaction ASAP.

Outside the store, you stop and take a deep breath and consider what you have just gotten away with. Conscious thought. You peer down the sidewalk. At the other end of the shopping center is a little African restaurant. There are tall, skinny, deeply black men congergated outside the establishment. Timmies. The place is called *Okru* or *Okru's Kitchen* or something like that. You walked by there once and looked at the menu posted on the door. You really couldn't make much sense of it, but it had faded-out pictures of some of the dishes. There was one thing they had that looked like a bowl of red spaghetti sauce with a boiled egg floating in the middle of it. A whole boiled egg just floating in a lake of red. It looked awful.

You get in your Escalade and head to a head shop (ha-ha). The name of the place is SMOKE. You've driven past it a million times, but you've never been inside. It's right up the street from where you live in a little strip mall nestled between a tanning parlor (called TAN) and a nail salon (called NAIL).

You park in front of the nail salon, because you don't want anybody to see your vehicle parked outside a head shop. You sit there and think a minute. And what you think is: SMOKE. TAN. NAIL. CUNT. Then you think about what you are doing here. You used to smoke herb when you were in college, back when you were your own person. You smoked quite a bit of it, in fact. But that was a long time ago. You have not been your own person in a long long time. You dropped out of college after that first year. When Mike got you pregnant. Barefoot, pregnant, and uneducated. That's how he liked his women. MIKE.

Anyway, you didn't want to smoke dope while you were pregnant. You aren't trash. You weren't then, anyway. And then it seemed like you stayed pregnant so much you just kind of forgot about smoking pot and getting high. Plus, Mike didn't approve of it and why make waves? A marriage is a partnership. Give and take. That was your thought process back then. Today, your thought process is that you want to get high. Good-n-high. This pot you have found is like a gift from God. Like God is telling you He wants you to enjoy life and be your own self, even if it's just for a little bit. Divine intervention is the only way you could get high these days, because you wouldn't have any idea where to buy some grass. Your friends had either gone straight like you did, or they never got married and had kids, but they weren't your friends anymore, not even on Facebook. They were probably too busy getting high and having sex with Timmies and generally enjoying life by doing whatever the hell they wanted to do.

SMOKE is quiet inside. It is not what you were expecting. You figured there would be incense burning and Led Zeppelin or maybe some Kanye playing. But inside it is quiet as a church or a library or something. No incense smoldering. It is sterile inside. In fact, it is like a scientist's laboratory. Everything is glass. Pyrex.

You take a look at the girl behind the counter. A glassy-eyed little thing. High. In fact, you understand why there is no music playing, this poor girl is so high that music would be too much sensation for her to process. So she just sits there, perched on her stool like a fragile little bird.

The showcase is a smorgasbord of glass water pipes and hookahs and glass bowls in neon swirls. There is an atomizer or nebulizer or something that just kind of heats up the pot or transports it like that matter transportation device from *The Fly*. You're not sure exactly how it works. You just came in here to get a pack of rolling papers. Job 1.5's. You didn't know pot smoking had been taken over by scientists. There is one little shelf that holds a few things that aren't made out of glass. You see a metal chamber pipe—it has a little hollow place in the middle where you can store pot and get it resin-coated—and at least that looks familiar. Old fashioned. Then something else on the shelf catches your eye. It's a small wooden container that comes with a hollowed-out ceramic cigarette. A little card next to it says "One Hitter $17.95." You buy it.

You get home just about thirty minutes before the first bus, Jazmyn's, is supposed to get there. So you park the Escalade in your driveway and you sit there and get high.

The pot is in fat, sticky, dense buds. Purple and resinous. It smells like Christmas. Christmas on Funk Mountain. The odor is like a mixture of pine and something like sweaty feet. You tear one bud apart into tiny syrupy clumps. You come across only one seed and two small stems. You flick the seed and stems out the window. You take the little clumps of gummy pot and rub them between your thumb and forefinger and crumble them into the wooden dugout box. Once there is a decent amount inside, your fingers are sticky like you got violin rosin on your hands.

All you do then is dip the hollowed-out end of the ceramic cigarette into the dugout and twist it around in there until the little opening is packed with weed. This is exactly one hit of pot—hence the name. Now you just hold the other end of the cigarette to your lips, light the lighter, and suck. If anyone should happen to be looking, why it would just look like you were helping yourself to a cigarette. Perfect.

The hit goes down pretty smooth. You cough, but just a little bit. You go ahead and smoke another hit, and then put everything away. Two hits is plenty. You don't want to get too high. Not with the school bus due in twenty minutes now. The kids might smell it on you or ask why you're acting so funny. *Why are your eyes so red, Mommy?* That would just break your heart. You wish you hadn't smoked it now, but maybe it doesn't matter, because you don't really feel anything anyway. Probably the pot was old and had lost its potency. It was old and stale and that's why it smelled so funky. Might have gone through the wash or something. Hopefully it hadn't been contaminated with dry cleaning chemicals or anything like that. Maybe you would feel a little buzz and that would be nice. That would be enough. You will have had your moment of rebellion.

It did have a strong smell though, so you might need to get out of the car and walk around a little bit to air out your clothes. That's what you are about to do, but you think again about Ben and Mike Jr., and sweet little Jazmyn seeing you high and that thought just breaks your heart all over again. What were you thinking? You are their mother. They are just innocent children. It makes you feel bad. What are you doing? You can't act like this when you are somebody's mother. When you are somebody's mother, you have a duty to act right. For all you know, that pot could have been sprayed with DDT. The pesticide could be working its way through your system right now. Making you sick. That stuff is straight-up poison. It causes chromosomal damage. It triggers cancer cells and speeds up metastasis. It could be that later when you hugged your kids the DDT would be collected in the oil and sweat glands in your skin and it would be transferred to those children, poisoning them. Altering their DNA. Maybe just a little. Maybe just enough to cause autism or mental retardation. What have you done? You have put yourself and your children at risk. What were you thinking? My God, for all you know that pot was laced with PCP. You could lose your mind and just snap. Transform into a violent monster. Just snap and end up killing your own children and devouring them. Mike would lose his shit. It would be on the news and the crime scene and the blood and the yellow police tape and the toxicology report would show that you had PCP in your system and folks would say she was just a suburban housewife and the news people would let slip that you were on food stamps and maybe this woman was more deeply troubled than anyone realized.

That's when you realize that you are indeed high. You are having a panic attack and you are high. So very very high. You are higher than you have ever been in your life. You might be higher than any human being has ever been in the history of people getting high. You understand, deep within you, that God did not intend man to be this high. It's not Christian. All you can do at this point is plead the blood of Jesus and pray. All you can do is say Jesus take the wheel, I'm too high to drive. And He will take it. Jesus will take the wheel and get you through this.

It could be that pot was from some government program where they spent millions of taxpayer dollars to develop a special strain of the most potent marijuana they could ever grow. Made by deranged scientists and you do not want to be this high this high this high. And your thoughts are echoing in your brain and that scares the shit out of you. Echoing echoing echoing. And then you think CUNT CUNT CUNT. And no wonder that poor bird-girl in SMOKE wouldn't listen to any music. If that girl was anywhere near—even one percent of one percent—as high as you are right now, then that poor child was skating on the outer edges of reality and any sensory input could have pushed her over the edge. And she would be lost forever.

You hope none of the neighbors saw you. For all you know, they could have taken pictures of you and uploaded them onto the internet. *This is my neighbor getting high in her car. She's on food stamps.* You shouldn't do anything in this world unless you were prepared to have it photographed or videoed and put on YouTube.

Or it could be that they saw you and have already called the police and the police could be on their way here right now and you could be arrested right as your kids were getting off the bus. That would be awful awful

awful. Fucking echo. It doesn't bother you so much now. The echo is actually kind of funny. And you laugh about that and laugh and laugh and laugh.

Then you realize that if the police really are on their way, you need to get your shit together. So you take the one-hitter and the lighter and the bag of pot and put it under the floor mat. But that is too lumpy and obvious. So you pop the rear hatch and put everything in the little hidey hole back there where the jack is stored.

You get back in the front seat, and you feel much better now. Safe. Let the cops come. You were just smoking a cigarette. But what if they have drug sniffing dogs? They still can't get into your trunk without a search warrant. You're safe. Cool on Christ.

Then you remember the seed and two stems you tossed out the window. The dogs would smell that. But that was a long time ago and the wind probably blew it away. But what if the dogs found it? Right there on your driveway or blown into the lawn? Busted. That would be probable cause right there. Then you would have to allow the officers to search your vehicle and all would be lost.

So you get out and get down on your hands and knees and it takes a long long long time but you by-God find that tiny seed and those two little stems. Inspiration strikes and you tuck it all into the exhaust pipe of the Caddie, but for all you know a dog could still smell it in there, so you dig it back out (your fingers get sooty) and you run to the backyard and up to the shrub fence and you throw it into the neighbor's yard. Ha ha.

You climb back into the Escalade and realize that you have been messing around with all of this for a very long time, and you must have been so high that the bus came and you missed it. They won't let the little kids get off unless there is a parent there to receive them. The bus driver would have to take them back to school. And since you weren't inside to answer the phone (Mike didn't want you to have a cell phone) they couldn't reach you to see what's wrong. It could be that by now they have called Social Services and DFACS because the kids have been abandoned. They would make that call right off the bat because when Mike signed you up for food stamps, he signed the kids up for free lunches at school so they would have already identified your children as coming from a troubled home. And God damn Mike anyway for causing this mess. If he'd just let you get a cell phone like a normal person. He said those things cause brain cancer. And how you hear about people getting blown up at filling stations, pumping gas and talking on their cell phones. They make tiny little electric sparks, he says.

You key the ignition and get ready to drive up to the school to see just how bad this situation has gotten. But when you glance at the clock on the dash, you see that only seven minutes have passed since you got high. You still have thirteen minutes before the bus gets here. This is a huge relief. You decide to get the stuff back out and take one more hit off the one-hitter since you have time time time.

* * *

Pretty soon you were getting high every day. You would get high and then vacuum the carpet. You would get high and scrub the toilets. You would get high and watch *The Price is Right* at 11:30 in the morning. You would get high and eat a whole bag of Funyuns by yourself. When you were good-n-high, the Funyuns crunching in your jaws was like chewing on religious rocks. Like you were Fred Flintstone working at the quarry and reading Bible passages on your coffee break.

You got used to it. It didn't make you paranoid anymore like it did that first time. Not as much, anyway. After a while, it just kind of mellowed you out. Not always, though. In fact, sometimes the high was so intense, you either had to hand it over to The Lord, or you just had to bear down and work your way through it. And it was like manual labor, getting that high. Sometimes after spending your morning working your way through another high, you had to lie down in the afternoon. To recuperate. Getting high was hard work.

Even though it only takes only a very little bit of the pot to get you high, you have smoked so much that it is starting to run low.

You went back to the head shop, SMOKE. You got to talking to that little birdy girl who works there and it turns out she really was dangerously high that day you came in. She let on that there was some crazy potent "Miley Cyrus" weed going around and that must be what you got ahold of. A tiny pinch was all it took to put you out there on the cutting edge.

She took you under her wing (ha ha) and explained a lot of the stuff they had for sale there. The vaporizer that kind of cooks the marijuana without burning it and cuts down on all the harmful toxins that get released when you smoke it the regular way. And she showed you all those beautiful clear laboratory glass bongs with heavy beaker bottoms and snaky glass tubing and bubbling liquids. It was all very scientific. You ended up buying a Pyrex bong with a glass ash-catcher add-on with a percolator downflow stem and a showerhead diffuser on the pre-filter. Again, it was all very scientific and looked like something out of *Bride of Frankenstein*, like a mad scientist designed it.

You kept all your paraphernalia inside an empty Tide box hidden up in a cabinet over the washing machine in the basement. And every time you smoked some, you were aware of your supply getting lower and lower.

When you were getting close to running out of Miley Cyrus, you went back again to SMOKE. The sparrow girl was there and you talked to her about this-and-that. Just girl stuff. And you bought a pack of rolling papers and screens (neither of which you needed) and a new diffuser for your bong. You asked Birdy, real casual, girl-to-girl, if she could hook you up, but Jenny (that was her real name) got kind of stiff and made it perfectly clear that wasn't going to happen. You looked like a middle class suburban housewife, and you guessed that was probably what an undercover cop would look like too.

* * *

Your most favorite thing to do while buzzed is shop Goodwill. You just groove on it. Click click click. You always go through the clothes racks real careful, checking the pockets, hoping you'll get lucky again. So far you have found a still-sealed Trojan Magnum condom, a used tube of lipstick, and a five-dollar bill.

In housewares, you see the usual banged-up pots and pans and chipped glassware and waffle irons with busted hinges. But today you also see the cutest lidded hand-basket. Wicker. It could be Longaberger, you never can tell. You pick it up and are surprised by the weight. It's fairly heavy, ten or fifteen pounds. You open the top and see that it's a pre-stocked picnic basket. It's stacked with plates and silverware and wineglasses and coffee cups and a stainless steel thermos—all nestled inside and tucked under the split lid.

You have a brief fantasy of you and Mike lying on a grassy bank next to a peaceful stream, feeding each other grapes. Only it's Andre and not Mike.

You want to get the basket, for the future. As tangible proof of the life you could be living. Of what you could become. But not today. Today you are broke.

Your stash is running out. Almost gone now. Just a couple pinches of resinous green crumbs for you to experiment with. And you have no way of getting more. You'll have to shut down your laboratory. It's a shame, because you have really enjoyed getting high. It takes your mind off things. And now it's going to end. But you can't think about that right now. If you do, you'll go crazy. You'll think about that tomorrow. Because right now, right this minute, you are high. Good-n-high. Tomorrow will take care of itself. After all, tomorrow is another day.

And so you head over to the clothes racks and click through the hangers and groove on your buzz, and you see that the shirt is still there. The blood-red one that says CUNT on it. It has a green price tag, and green tag items are half price today. You are surprised the shirt is still here. But then again, what kind of person would buy something like that anyway? You think about that and think some more about it, and finally you decide that *you* are the kind of person who would buy something like that.

You are going to buy it. Except you can't. Mike has cut you off of cash. The Pyrex bong and all the doodads to go with it were not cheap. You had to withdraw cash to get it. Mike was pissed. The shirt wouldn't be much, but you are penniless. Like Scarlett O'Hara at the end of the Civil War. But you couldn't run home and make a CUNT shirt out of the curtains in the living room. And you couldn't use your bank card, because Mike would see you had been shopping at Goodwill.

You take the shirt and hanger to the dressing cubicle. You put the CUNT shirt on, and put the blouse you had been wearing onto the hanger. Then you go back to the sales floor and put that hanger on the rack. Click.

And there you are, walking through Goodwill in a shoplifted blood-red spaghetti-strap tank top that says CUNT in big black letters. On your way out, you stop by housewares and grab that handbasket, too. You look like some kind of porn-film prostitute version of *Little Red Riding Hood* as you stroll right out the front door with your stolen goods. Nobody stops you.

Outside, the sun is too bright. It hurts your eyes. You squint down the sidewalk to your left, and you see that same group of black men standing outside Okru's Kitchen. Tall skinny black men. Maybe they are contemplating whether or not to get a bowl of whole egg in blood sauce. And you look at those men and you think about the two pinches of Miley Cyrus left at home. You bet one of those men would know where you could get a dime bag or something. Maybe a quarter. But of course you don't have any money, so why take the risk? You doubt they even sell dime bags anymore. A dime bag probably costs a hundred dollars or something.

Then you remember how Mike said the Timmies use their food stamps to buy drugs and sex, and how the Timmie women were defined by their sexual organs. You touch your pants pocket and feel the EBT card snug in there.

You have your CUNT shirt on and your handbasket dangling at your side. You imagine the dirty sidewalk is really a path in the dark woods. And you are just traipsing along it. Like Little Red Riding Hood off to match wits with the Big Bad Wolf.

Your EBT has $526.00 on it.

You start off down the sidewalk in your red tank top.
Toward the Timmies.

A Story About A Dog (Told From The Dog's Point of View)

Boy. Boy. Boy. Boy. Boy. Boy. Boy. Boy. Boy. Boy. Boy. Boy. Boy. Boy. Boy. Boy. Boy. Boy. Boy. Boy. Boy. Boy. Boy. Boy. Boy. Boy. Boy.

Move. Move. Move. Boy move. Go. Boy move. Go. Boy move go. Go. Go. Go. Outside! Outside! Outside! Outside! Out! Out! Out! Out! Out!

Smell. Smell. Pee. Pee. Smell. Pee. Smell pee. Smell Pee. SOME GODDAMN DOG HAS BEEN PEEING IN MY YARD! SOME GODDAMN DOG HAS BEEN PEEING IN MY YARD! My yard. My yard. Pee. Must pee. Must Pee. Must pee here. Must pee here now. Now must pee. Here. Pee. Yes. Yes. Yes...

Boy? Boy? Boy? Smell. Boy? Smell. Yes. Run. Run. Run. Run. Smell. Run. Run. Smell. Run. Boy. Boy. Boy. Boy. Boy. Boy. Boy. Boy. Boy. Boy, boy, boy, boy, boy, boy, boy, boy, boy, boy, boy, boy, boy.

New yard. New yard. New house. New yard. (BAD BOY.) (BAD BOY) (BAD BOY.) Boy? Boy? Smell. Smell. Pee. Smell pee. Smell pee. THAT GODDAMN DOG! THAT

GODDAMN DOG! Fix him! Fix him! FIX THAT GODDAMN DOG! Pee. Pee. Pee. Yes.

Boy? Boy? Boy? Smell. Smell. Boy? Boy? Run. Run. Run. Smell. Run. Smell. Run. Boy. Boy. Boy. Boy. Boy. (BAD BOY.) Boy. Boy. Boy. Boy. Boy. (BAD BOY.) Boy. Go. Go. Go. Go. Go. Go. Go. Go. Go. Go. Go. Go. Go. Go. Go. Go. New yard. New yard. New house. New yard. Smell. Smell. Good. Smell. Good smell. Good. No smell. No smell good. Good no smell. Pee.

Boy? Boy? Boy? Boy? Boy? Boy? (No smell.) Boy? Boy? Boy? Boy? Boy? Boy? Boy? Boy? boy? boy? boy? boy? boy? boy? boy?.... boy?.... boy?.... boy?.... boy?.... boy?.... sleep.

Boy! Boy! Boy! Boy! Boy! Boy! Boy. Boy. Boy. Boy. Boy. (BAD BOY.) Boy. Boy. Boy. Boy. Boy. (Girl.) Boy. Boy. Boy. Boy. (BAD BOY.) Boy. (Girl.) Boy. Go. Go. Go. Go. Go. Go. Go. Go. Go. Go. Go. Go. Go. Go. Go. Go. Go. Go. Go. Go. Go. Go.

Woods. Woods! Woods! Go in woods! Go in. Smell. Wonderful. Wonderful. Smell. Wonderful smell. Run. Run. Alone. Run. Alone. Run. Alone. Run. Run. Run. Run. Run. Joy. Run. Run. Joy. Alone. Joy. Run. Joy. Joy. Joy. Smell. Smell. Roll. Roll. Roll. Roll. Joy! Joy! Joy! Joy! Roll! Roll! Roll! Roll! Joy. Roll. Joy. Roll. joy.... LISTEN! LISTEN! LISTEN! Bird!? BIRD! BIRD! JOY! Run. Run. Run. Run. Run. Run. Run. Run. Run. Run. Stop. Rest. Rest. Rest, rest, rest, rest, rest, rest, rest, rest, rest, rest.... rest.... rest.... rest.... BIRD! Run. Run. Run. Run. Run. Run. Run. Stop. Rest. Rest, rest, rest, rest,

rest, rest, rest.... rest.... rest.... sun.... rest.... sun.... rest.... sun.... sleep.

LISTEN! Scream!? Listen! Listen! Boy? Boy? Boy? Boy? Scream! (Girl.) Run.

Boy. (BAD BOY.) (Girl.) Boy? (Girl?) Hurt. Smell. Hurt. Smell. Hurt smell. (Girl.) Smell. Heat. Blood. Sex. Heat. Blood. Sex. Heat Blood. Sex. Smell. Smell. Smell. Heat. Blood. Sex. Heat Blood Sex. Death. HeatBloodSex. Death. HEATBLOODSEX. DEATH. HEATBLOODSEXDEATH! Boy?

Smell boy. Smell boy. HeatBloodSex. Boy smell heatBloodSex. Smell. Smell. (BAD BOY.) Smell. Smell (BAD BOY.) HeatBloodSex. Badness. Heat. Blood. Sex. Death. Badness. KICK. Hurt! Hurt! Hurt! Hurt! Hurt! Hurt! KICK. Hurt! Hurt! Hurt! Hurt! Hurt! Hurt. Hurt. Hurt. Hurt. Hurt. Hurt. (BAD BOY.)

Boy. Boy. Boy. Boy. Boy. Boy. Boy? Boy. Boy? Pet. Pet. Pet. Yes. Me. Pet. Yes. Joy. Joy. Joy. Yes, yes, yes, yes, yes, yes. Pet me. Boy! Boy!

Go. Go. Go. Go. Go. Go. Go. Go. Go. Go. Go. Go. Go. Go. Go. Go. Go. Go. Go. Go. Go. Go. Go. Go. Go. Go. Go. Go. Go. Go. Go. Go.

Boy. (BAD BOY.)

EULA SHOOK

It was a plain, polished granite slab that sat flush to the freshly wrenched, red Georgia earth. On the left, it said:

HUBERT SHOOK
OCT 1, 1939—SEPT 29, 2013

And to the right:

EULA SHOOK
APRIL 8, 1942—

Eula found that dash worrisome. If they'd just left off the dash, then maybe it would set right with her.

The funeral director had called it a companion marker. To be purchased "pre-need." Although, for Hubert, two days dead by then, it was really more of a now-need.

The death man had dark eyes. Eula had never met a blue-eyed funeral director. Not once.

He had said, as though reading from a catalogue, "A companion marker reflects the bond between a man and wife, so that the two will be remembered as a couple for as long as history is kept."

And although she was not typically prone to flights of fancy, this made Eula imagine an apocalyptic future in which hardscrabble survivors might find her and Hubie's tombstone and know that they had been made one in the eyes of God.

Still, it was morbid to see your name on a granite slab, and it wasn't until the sable-eyed, sable-suited death merchant mentioned the cost savings of purchasing pre-need—her date of death would be added later for "a nominal fee"—that she agreed to it. With their son, Jerry, dead and buried in the Marietta National Cemetery, there would be no family left behind to be burdened with final costs. Still. It was best to save money where you could. And Eula found herself wanting to please the death seller. She had always been drawn to men with eyes of murk.

Now, two weeks after the funeral, the temporary marker had been taken up, and this permanent one (*for as long as history is kept*) had been put down. Eula looked at her own grave. It still didn't set right. She looked again at her husband's born and died dates. Hubert always did love fall the best. And he damn near held on till his birthday. Eula and Betty had both decided that's what he was doing. Holding on until October first. But he didn't make it. No. The throat cancer took him. The Good Lord called him home.

But that wasn't true. That was just what they told everybody. That God had sent for him. That The Good

Lord blessed us and took Hubie home. But Hubie took his own self home.

He'd been lingering for some time. The Hospice nurse had told Eula and Betty that it happens like that. They linger. It was hard on the family mostly. That nurse was the one that put it in Eula's head that maybe Hubert was aiming to check out on his birthday. She'd seen it before. She'd seen them hold on until their wedding anniversary, or their child's graduation, or until their favorite show was playing on TV. *Andy Griffith's on. I can let go.* That nurse was full of similar observations.

All he was, was a morphine-addicted skeleton. Monster-movie sutures draped from ear to ear to ear like a necklace. As though a slow-witted child had tried to carve a jack-o-lantern and put the mouth six inches too low.

They linger.

The cancer had spread into his brain and who knew where all else. And Eula had prayed to Jesus Christ every night not to let him linger, to take him. She prayed that He would be merciful and take Hubie now. Right that minute. Don't make him wait. It was a shameful way to live. Soaking in his own waste. Playing in it. Smearing his feces all over himself. He'd been a proud—not vain—man who took care in his appearance, kept his hair oiled and his shirt tucked even if he'd spent all day tending the hogs. So she prayed.

He got to where he got real active at night. Restless. He would sleep and dream his Dilaudid dreams by day, but at night he was up and talking and running the top sheet through his fingers like a nervous little girl playing with her petticoat. Talking. Plain talking. Maybe not as clear as a bell, but lucid. Vibrating what was left of his vocal cords. And just a-talking. The information-laden nurse said Hubie was sundowning. Where they perk up and come to life at night. She'd seen it before. (Eula figured if Hubie clucked like a Rhode Island Red and laid an egg, this woman would say she'd seen it before).

The nurse said sundowning usually lasted two or three days, then they passed. Well good, Eula thought. She sat up with Hubie and talked with him the same way they had talked as teenagers. Easy. They talked easy. He told her about the time Homer Smith fell into the scalding vat at the slaughterhouse. Boiled him alive. How he could still hear the man-screams sometimes. And he told Eula about the time J.T. Thompson had his legs severed in the industrial meat grinder at Douglas Meat Packing Plant. How he was pretty sure old J.T.'s legs ended up in a batch of liver cheese and shipped across the country. Hubie wouldn't eat baloney, or hot dogs, or Vienna sausages, or any processed meats. He'd seen too much.

He told her about how pretty his mama was, and how he thought she was an angel like the color plates in their family Bible. That his father was a mean son of a bitch. That he caught three ten-pound bass out of Turner's pond, and Mr. Turner chased him off his land firing rock salt at him. How he had his eye on that Eula Graybeal. Pretty little thing.

He talked to her like they were friends. Hubert and

Eula had not been friends in a very long time. They'd been husband and wife.

The sundowning came and went and Hubie held on.

They linger.

The man was stubborn. Eula kept her eye on the calendar. He never celebrated his birthday when he was fully alive and healthy, so why he would be shooting for it now was beyond her reckoning.

Then, at 10:30 in the morning on September 29th, Hubert came down the stairs and walked in on Eula in the kitchen. She was just sitting at the table having a cup of decaffeinated Nescafe. No need in brewing a whole pot when it was just her drinking it. He scared Eula when he walked in. She had not heard him approaching, because Hubie only weighed eighty-five pounds, so his weight had not been sufficient to make the floor joists squeak. And, in any regard, Hubert Shook had not been out of bed in three weeks. His walking days were behind him. Or so she thought. That's what the helpful Hospice nurse had said. But there he stood. Like something that ought not be alive.

He did not speak to her, but held her eyes with his. It made Eula feel like she'd been caught doing something wrong. Something nasty. She was too surprised to speak. And as they looked at each other across the kitchen, something came out of Hubert's nose. It was black as tar and as thick as a man's finger. To Eula, it looked darkly alive. Like a parasite that had been living inside Hubie and was ready to get out while the getting was good. Of course it was the cancer. His body so used up and stove in that even the cancer was fleeing it. And she could see the torment in Hubie's eyes. Pain that no narcotic could ever numb.

And he lurched to the cabinet drawer directly under the Amana Radarange. The drawer where they kept the gun. A .22 caliber revolver had been in that drawer as long as Eula could remember. Since before she even knew there was even such a thing as microwave ovens. Hubert kept it handy there because he liked to sit on the front porch and pick off squirrels that were bad to get into the bird feeders, and the raccoons that would tip over the garbage cans at night.

Hubert raised the bore to his temple and put a bullet into his brain. While Eula watched. It was loud. But the funny thing was that the mess wasn't nearly as bad as Eula would have thought. The TV shows made it look like brains and blood and bone fragments would spray across everything and spackle the ceiling too. But it wasn't that bad. Probably because the gun watn't but a itty bitty .22.

She called Betty first. Betty was Eula's best friend and her bus monitor too. Betty had sat with Eula in the hospital when the breast cancer took Eula's sister, Mary Alice. Cancer was bad.

Betty told Eula to hang up the phone and call 911. So that's what she did. She told the dispatcher there wasn't a number on the mailbox, but just look for the house with a yellow school bus parked in the front yard. Under the black walnut tree.

In the ten minutes she had to herself before either the

ambulance or Betty would get there, Eula sat in the kitchen with Hubie and finished her coffee. She told him she was sorry he was dead, but she was glad he was gone. Glad he was out of his pain. But she was also glad he was dead because she had been ready to have leave of him. She thought saying that out loud would relieve her of the burden of guilt she had been carrying, but it didn't. There was no feeling of the lancing of a wound. No release. So she went on. She told him that she'd been tired of him. Sick of him. And she was sure the feeling had been mutual. And that was okay. She forgave him. And she asked him to forgive her too.

Still, she didn't feel any better. Something was wrong inside her.

After that, she prayed in silence for Hubie's soul. It was just a gesture, because Eula was pretty sure suicides went to hell.

And now, two weeks later, she nodded her final approval of the grave marker. Although she did not approve. Not at all.

She kept eyeing that blank spot after the dash.

The death man smiled at Eula and held her in his eyes of murk.

The call from the doctor's office had been like a mean joke.

The day had started off good, though. When she went outside early that morning to warm up the bus, the air was perfumed from the black walnut tree—sweet and tangy, like something boiled in a cast iron pot at the county fair. The boughs were heavy with the ripe green fruit. An overnight rain storm had sent many of them to the ground. They were the size of crabapples, and split open under Eula's shoes, spewing out black, spore-like flesh. She brushed them from where they had collected in the wiper well of her bus. It was a wonder the squirrels hadn't got to them and carried them off. Maybe with their executioner having turned the gun on himself, they would feel more comfortable and come get these that were littering the yard.

She'd run her morning route. It had been a good run. Uneventful. The morning runs were usually smooth. The children were still groggy from getting up early, and they had crusty sleep in the corners of their eyes. The inside of the bus was cozy warm and smelled like instant oatmeal and Sugar Frosted Flakes and Log Cabin syrup. It was still dark outside. The morning runs generally went smooth.

She got back home around 10:30 and had a cup of Nescafe at the kitchen table like she always did. After that, she went to the living room couch and lay down to take a little nap. She put a dish towel over the cushion so the hairspray from her hair wouldn't stain the fabric. She was just drifting off when the phone rang. Probably a telemarketer. They were so bad anymore it made you afraid to answer your own phone. She was aware of caller ID and cordless phones and cell phones and all of that, but Eula still used the hard-wired rotary phone that had been in the house even longer than Hubie's .22. She sat up, lifted the receiver, and spoke a suspicious hello into the mouthpiece.

It was the doctor's office.

They weren't supposed to give you that kind of news over the phone. Even Eula knew that they were supposed to tell you that you needed to come in and review your test results with Dr. Parker. Maybe they figured Eula was so old that the news of her imminent death wouldn't be as disturbing to her as it would be to a young person. A young person with their whole life in front of them might become depressed or do something crazy.

But no, the nurse said that the ovarian cancer had reached her liver. Stage four. And she would need to make an appointment with Dr. Parker to discuss treatment options and would you like me to connect you to the scheduling desk?

Eula said she would call back later. She sat on the couch and imagined a finger-thick cord of black cancer worming its way out of her woman parts. She could not let that happen. She prayed that wasn't what The Lord had in store for her.

Why was there so much cancer in the world today? What are we doing to make this disease so common? It was like the world itself had cancer. The eating kind.

Eula never did get her nap in that day. She paced a lot. Walking from one end of the house to the other, like a cancer worm was tracking her. She pulled out the family photo album. There was Hubert, just a shoat, crew cut, his teeth not yet stained from the plug of Beech Nut he always kept in his lower jaw. There was Hubert and his brother Reid pouring the concrete foundation for this house. Hubert had built this house himself. The plumbing, the carpentry, the wiring, brickwork, roofing. All of it. The man was talented. Hubert was dead now, but his house still stood.

And there was Jerry. Their son. He was dead now too. There was Jerry in the front yard on his Big Wheel. The black walnut tree was a lot smaller back then and there was still grass in the yard. She remembered Jerry rode that Big Wheel until the black plastic wheels just disintegrated. As a Cub Scout. As a football player. With his prom date. Pretty girl. Eula couldn't remember her name now. She'd come to the funeral, though. There he was with the harsh shorn head of a new recruit. He looked so young and strong like life was just busting out of him. Dead.

And there was Eula herself. She had been pretty in her way. Dainty, almost frail. A world away from the solid thing she was now. As the harried mother of a newborn. As the mother of a toddler, lines starting to set in around her eyes. Jerry was a handful. There she was reading nursery rhymes to Jerry. *This is the cat that killed the rat that ate the malt that lay in the house that Jack built.* There she was, stouter, after the news about Jerry. The lines set in permanently now. The life gone from her eyes. *This is the maiden, all forlorn.*

She was dead now, too.

Eula cried some. She didn't care nothing about dying. But she thought of herself lying in bed, digging BM out of her own rectum and smearing it in her hair, and the hospice nurse smiling and saying "that's the way they do sometimes. I've seen it before."

They linger.

She thought of the death man, the twinkle in his sooty eyes as he used a hammer and chisel to fill in that awful blank space after the dash.

A little bit after noon, she put the album away and went to the kitchen. To the cabinet that held the microwave. That sat above the drawer. That stored the gun. That held the bullet. That finished Hubie. *This is the cat that killed the rat that ate the malt that lay in the house that Jack built.* And in the bottom of that cabinet, Eula found the corn liquor that Hubert kept stored there. It was in a wide-mouth Ball jar. Homemade. He kept it filled from a jug in the basement. He made it down there. Kept a still. Eula had seen it. He had bags of corn meal and cans of yeast. Bags of sugar and malt. *This is the malt that lay in the house that Hubie built.* She stayed away from all that. He only made it once, maybe twice a year. It was a wonder he never went blind.

Eula unscrewed the metal ring and pried off the lid. She brought her nose down to the jar and sniffed. Her head rocked back. She brought the jar to her lips and tasted it. It was like dipping your tongue in lye. It was like her mouth was telling her every way it knew how not to subject it to that poison.

She forced it down. Medicine. *This is the rat that ate the malt.* It helped. The fire in her mouth became a fire in her throat that became a fire in her chest that became a fire in her stomach that radiated through her whole body. *This is the liquor that burned the mouth that seared the esophagus that bore the cancer that ate the body that Hubie built.*

Eula shuddered against the cold fire. She wanted more and decided to take the liquor on a spoon. She used a good solid stainless steel spoon that was bigger than a table spoon. It was her favorite spoon. She used it to dip and eat ice cream. It was probably silly to have a favorite spoon.

She got the photo album out again, taking spoonfuls of moonshine as she browsed. It didn't hurt as much this time. She started wishing for a cigarette. She hadn't smoked since 1976 when she was pregnant with Jerry. Kent Golden Lights. That's what she smoked and wanted now.

After a while, she took the spoon out of the canning jar and laid it on a crochet doily on the coffee table. She sipped from the jar. She felt okay. Happy, even.

When Eula looked up at the clock, it was 2:30. She had to be at the school by 2:45 for her three o'clock run.

When she left her house (the house that Hubie built) she left the door unlocked, and in her purse she carried something that belonged to Hubie, and in her womb she carried something that belonged to her alone.

Eula made it to Joe Frank Harris Intermediate School on time and pulled into her empty slot in the loading zone. Usually, the drivers slid into their slanted spaces and opened up their doors and driver's windows so they could talk and gossip. But today, Eula kept her Wayne International sealed tight. She just stared straight ahead and never even made eye contact with her fellow drivers.

At three o'clock, when first-grader Nathan Tattnall tapped at the loading door, Eula reached forward and lifted the thumb clasp

That released the handle

That opened the door

That let in the students

That trusted the widowed driver

That bore a dark secret in her womb

That was numbed with the moonshine

The was stored in the cabinet

That held the microwave

That sat above the drawer

That stored the revolver

That held the bullet

That brought down the house that Hubie built.

Russell Roxburry, Wanda Lumpkin, and Mandy Slade were the last ones on the bus. They were fifth graders, ten years old. The third and fourth graders loaded earlier. Nathan Tattnall, seven, seated in the first seat to the driver's right, leaned across the aisle and tugged at Eula's sleeve.

"Miss Eula, are you sad?"

"Nathan, no sweetie, I ain't sad. Why would you say that?"

"Cause you cryin'."

Eula looked up to the oblong overhead mirror and

was surprised to see her face wet, eyes red. She didn't feel sad though.

Eula reached over and pulled the Wayne's manual jack-knife handle. The folding door closed with a loud mechanical squeak. The bus was old. Sturdy, but old. Eula pulled forward out of her slot and into the exit lane, as she had ten thousand times before. Today she clipped the protruding corner of the loading zone sidewalk, rolled a rear tire over it. The bus shook and rocked the students left and right. It was fairly common for the drivers to clip this concrete corner that stuck out too far. Eula herself never had.

She waved to the officer on traffic duty just as she always did, and pulled the twenty-foot Wayne International onto Highway 41. The Wayne took the turn too wide and spent too long in the oncoming lane. Eula maneuvered the steering wheel hand-over-hand to get the bus back in the correct lane before it hit the white SUV that headed the line of stopped traffic. She overcorrected and the bus ended up going onto the soft shoulder and into the shallow roadside drainage ditch. One of the first-grade girls (Belinda Edwards, who was high-strung anyway) screamed, but Eula maneuvered the Wayne cleanly out of the culvert and back onto Northbound 41.

The bus was quiet for a Friday afternoon. All the children were watching Eula. She had never so much as taken them over a pothole before, so they wanted to see what she would do next.

What she did next was to angle her arm down to her

big brown pocketbook and reach herself out the greatly depreciated Ball jar

thatsatinthecabinet

thatwasunderthedrawer

thatheldthegun

thatfiredthebullet

thatbroughtdownthehousethatHubiebuilt.

The bus was so quiet that everybody could plainly hear the metal-on-glass of Eula unscrewing the top off the jar. She held the open container out to Nathan, but he shook his head and launched into a snotty crying spell. Eula had always found the boy to be a little effeminate. Sissy. But she tried not to judge a child so young. Still, it was plain. No telling what kind of man he might grow up to be. What kind of house he would build. What would ultimately bring that house down.

Eula took a good long swallow of the corn liquor. It still burned, but she didn't mind it as much now. It lit up her whole face with warmth. She replaced the lid, securing it with the aluminum ring, and as she reached the jar back down to her purse, the Wayne International sailed through a four-way stop without slowing down even one little bit.

It was so quiet. Eula was tempted to turn on the radio, but she didn't approve of popular music for little kids like that. It used to be songs had innuendo and double meanings, but now they just come right out and say shake your boombah and put it in my face. She would like to play Christian music for them, but she got reported for that one time.

Mandy Slade's was the first stop. The only stop on Stockmar Road. Eula engaged the flashing yellow caution lights, glided to a stop in front of the Slade's red-brick ranch style house, and extended the lighted stop sign. (Cars are supposed to stop—if they safely can—when the yellow cautions start flashing. Lots of people didn't know or didn't care and would speed up to get past the bus so they wouldn't get stuck waiting. Eula could understand this and tried not to let it bother her. But she kept a notepad close by to write down the tag number of any vehicle that passed her once the stop sign swung out).

Eula waited for Mandy to gather her backpack and stride to the front. Eula opened the glass curtain door and waved to Mrs. Slade who was standing at the end of the driveway. The real young kids had to have someone waiting on them or Eula couldn't let them off. Margie Slade waved back, and Eula wondered if the woman knew how bad that Clorox dye job was ruining her hair. She looked like a scarecrow.

Eula lumbered the Wayne back into motion. In the side mirror, she spied Mrs. Slade running behind the bus, her face pinched red, her lifeless hair scattering in bleachy wisps. The woman was waving her down. These people. These people were always wanting something.

Eula sighed and stopped the bus. She opened the door and waited. Mrs. Slade climbed up to the second step and looked back at the scared, quiet children. Then she looked at Eula, her face painted with grave concern.

"Eula, are you all right?"

"Hey, Margie. I'm fine. Why?"

"Why?"

Eula blinked at her. She was having trouble following.

"Why, is because you just took out my mailbox."

Eula blinked several more times. "I did? Are you sure? Maybe the mailman. Or teenagers."

"It wasn't teenagers. Look, it's right there in the middle of the road. You dragged it twenty feet."

"Well, my Lord."

There was a moment of silence. Perhaps for the fallen mailbox.

Margie scanned the seats again and asked, "Where's Betty?"

"Female trouble."

"Oh."

"Margie, I believe your mailbox was already down before I got here."

"No, ma'am. No. I saw you snag it on the bumper. Snapped it off at the base."

"We'll have to agree to disagree."

"Eula, I want you to do something for me. I want you to breathe in my face."

"Breathe in your face?"

"Yes. Please."

"I will not."

"Just blow in my face."

"Margie, you've lost your mind. You're not allowed on this bus. Get off."

"Not until you blow in my face."

"No, ma'am. Get off. You're breaking the law."

"I will not get off this bus until you breathe in my face."

Eula saw the woman meant it, so she reached out and shoved Margie Slade backwards. Hard. The woman fell back a step, pinwheeled, was still falling, and one of her hands caught the vertical steel pole. Before Margie could completely right herself, Eula pulled the jack knife door handle, and the folding mechanism caught Mrs. Slade, pinning her half on and half off the bus. Eula put the Wayne in motion, built up some speed, then swerved the bus back and forth across Stockmar Road, trying to shake Margie off like a booger stuck on her finger. It worked. Margie took a tumble. Rolled into some blackberry bushes like she was Br'er Rabbit.

The kids were coming out of their awe now, whimpering. Low grade terror. It couldn't be helped.

Once the Wayne International was back on 41, Eula took another swallow from the shine jar. To settle her nerves. She turned on to Cheatham Hill and into the Legacy Isle subdivision. Three of the kids were supposed to get off here. She saw the mothers waiting, but before the bus came to a complete stop, Eula took her foot off the brake and stabbed the gas pedal. These buses had more get up and go than most people would think. She just couldn't let these children off with them crying and snotting.

In the side view, Eula could see the perplexed parents, their heads bobbing, fingers pointing. She turned on the radio. Full-on gospel.

She heard kids calling out *Miss Eula!* and *what's*

wrong? And *please stop please.* She flew right on past their stops. She couldn't hear them. She had other things on her mind. Eula was drunk.

She turned around in her seat, wanting to see the faces of the children without the filter of the mirror. As she did, the bus drifted across 41 and off the opposite shoulder. The Wayne slid down into a young stand of loblolly pine. The limbs slapped the bus thwap thwap thwap thwap thwap like a playing card on bicycle spokes. Eula thought: *Wheeeee!* Some of the passenger windows were open, and the tender green limbs sprung through and were immediately snapped off due to the bus's high speed. Boughs of clean young pine were flying through the Wayne International's interior. The fresh sap released through the violent amputation filled the bus with a sharp clean scent that was somewhere between turpentine and Christmas.

The children were outright screaming now. Some of them hysterical. Something was bad wrong with the world today. They were running up and down the aisle. Pandemonium. Russell Roxbury had his hands to his head, elbows poked out, in a cartoonish image of consternation. It was downright comical.

Eula righted the bus back onto the two-lane and told them to hush up. She didn't usually snap at the children like that, but they were really being babies today. This was fun and they didn't even know it. Their parents kept them so keyed up and high strung. This was really just an adventure.

Eula got the bus rolling smooth down 41. It felt good.

Music was on the radio. A choir singing *At the End of the Road*, talking about how sweet relief from all care will be waiting for me there when I come to the end of the road. Eula reckoned that was where this trip was going to end, at the end of the road. She felt good. The music sounded good. She loved driving the bus. She had been on this road a long long time. It had been a long life. She had seen a lot of things change. Change. Change could be hard. Children with pink hair and black fingernails, baby girls in makeup and bare stomachs, pants that sat on their pubic bone—these were just children.

She saw that they had their little cell phones out now. Calling people and taking pictures. Children with little Dick Tracy gadgets. Their little phones and games and movie cameras all of it hooked up to the outer space thing. They were calling their parents. They were taking movies of her. Although Eula didn't know the word "upload" she knew that's what they were doing. Taking movies of her and putting them up there in outer space for everybody to see. She had seen these videos on the news. That story about the poor bus monitor with them nasty-mouthed children poking her rolls of fat and filming her until she cried. Eula wasn't going to cry. She was smarter than she let on. She knew damn well the outer space thing was called the Internet; it just suited her mind to play the old lady sometimes. And she knew all their nasty words too. The F word. All of them. She just chose not to wallow in such.

In the side mirror, she saw a Chevrolet Equinox fall in behind the bus. It was Margie Slade, her scarecrow hair flying in the breeze. Margie was on her cell phone too. Eula could see bleeding scratches on the woman's face and forehead. From the blackberry briars. Then a Cobb County sheriff pulled alongside Mrs. Slade. He waved her off then hit his lights and siren. But Margie stayed right alongside him. She was mad, probably.

Eula's gaze fell to the Georgia state flag decal mounted in the lower corner of the windshield. The old one with the rebel emblem. All the buses had it at one time. Then they changed the flag. Said it was racist. Eula got a letter in the mail from the superintendent of Cobb County schools. Said remove the flag decal. But she refused. She was proud of her heritage. She didn't hate. She wasn't a racist. Didn't believe the flag was racist. Didn't believe that no more than the man in the moon. She voted for Governor Sonny Perdue because he said he would bring the flag back. But he didn't. Sonny lied.

The South was disappearing. Hell, it was gone. It was up there in outer space with everything else. And when she was dead, they could forget about laying her in the dirt with Hubie, they could just shoot her out there in space too. It used to be people were proud to be from the South, and now they acted like they was ashamed of it.

The Sheriff's cruiser was angling up in front of her, trying to slow her down, cut her off, stop her. Lights going off like blue flashbulbs, siren giving her a headache and drowning out her gospel. But she just swerved around him, like he was nothing. And she could see there were more parents back there, joining the chase, lining up in their white SUVs. They loved those SUVs. Loved 'em as much as they loved their cell phones.

It was all just too much. Too much of everything. Eula stopped the bus. Stopped right in the middle of Northbound Highway 41, and took a last pull off the liquor jar. It was empty now. Thank you, Hubie. She wasn't stopped but just a minute, but that was long enough for things to start sliding away from her. Russell Roxbury and Wanda Lumpkin got the rear emergency exit open and jumped on out. Most all the fourth and fifth graders followed them out. Not Nathan Tattnall, though. Him and all the other real young ones stayed on the bus. They trusted Miss Eula.

She could see parents popping out of their shiny vehicles and scooping up their kids. And she could see the sheriff's deputy sidling up the bus on the driver's side. He had on his brown and tan uniform and his ranger hat. Eula could see he was being real cautious like she was dangerous or something. He was edging along the side of the bus, his fingers playing over the grip of his service pistol.

Eula leaned out the window and threw the Ball jar at him. It hit him right in the face. She saw his hands go up to cover himself and some blood was there too. She called him a motherfucker and took off.

The ramp for the interstate was right up ahead. I-75. She wanted to feel some wind in her hair. Maybe cruise on down to Atlanta. Look for the gold dome and go shake the hand of the man who ousted Sonny Perdue. Or maybe hit him in the eye. He wasn't going to bring back her flag either. And then she realized that she never gave a damn about that flag anyway. It was just something to go on about. None of it mattered. Nathan Tattnall was weeping. A steady stream. Like a little girl. Eula didn't understand why there was so much anger in her. There was the ramp to the interstate. The bus flattened two metal signs that said WRONG WAY and DO NOT ENTER in red capital letters.

It was fun dodging the oncoming cars. She did it for a long time. At first she thought it was them moving in the wrong direction, after a while she realized they were moving forward and she was moving backward. It was probably dangerous, but she could handle it. She thought about white SUVs and cell phones and dirty words and text messages and satellites in outer space and her little bus moving the wrong way, against all of it. She thought of children dressed up like harlots and thugs and she wondered if kids today would ever know the simple pleasures of childhood, like Hansel and Gretel and Mother Goose and nursery rhymes. Then she saw that an eighteen-wheeler loaded with gasoline (actually nine thousand gallons of isobutane, the driver would later tell the *Atlanta Journal-Constitution*) was bearing down on her. She thought of the fireball that would result if she maintained her collision course. They'd probably be able to see it from out there in space. But the rig driver saw her and hit his brakes. The tanker jackknifed. It went into an oblong skid that covered four lanes of the interstate. Eula thought of a joke the kids liked to tell each other. The punchline was *crispy critters.* She kept her eyes open. The tanker continued its skid, turning. It slid right on past the bus like pistons packed in grease sliding next to each other. It was that close. It kept on sliding and went off the interstate and into a stand of crape myrtles.

She could see there were several sheriff's deputies back there now, sirens screaming at her. A little trail of white SUVs. And looked like a news van from one of the Atlanta stations. Eula was going to make the news. They would ask her *what were you thinking?* That's what they would want to know. She had no idea what her answer would be.

Eula gradually noticed that she wasn't dodging oncoming traffic anymore, which was a disappointment because she really liked doing that. They must have shut down the interstate on her account. They could do that fast nowadays in this world where people blew up buildings and spread poison gas.

There was a helicopter up in the sky, thumping away, trying to get her attention. She wished she could tell them that she didn't want to hurt anybody, that she had no poison to spread. And she saw that up ahead they had set up some kind of blockade all lit up and flashing big as Christmas morning. Police cars and ambulances, little armored tank things and what looked like a prison bus. All strewed across the blacktop like game pieces across a Monopoly board. Even Monopoly was different today with plastic credit cards instead of cash money.

Eula reckoned she would not be passing Go today. She was at the end of the road.

She didn't know what to do next. She looked over to sissy boy Nathan, but he was curled up into a tight ball on his seat. Reminded Eula of a roly poly, protecting himself. The other little kids back there didn't have any suggestions either. Jazmyn Hughes. Lakesha Moon. Jeff Cain. Gail Stevens. She loved them. They couldn't help how their parents raised them.

Eula stopped the bus. Because she loved them. And this made her realize that she loved Hubert too. That she really did love him. This surprised her. And it made her realize that if she really did love him, then he probably really did love her too. He was the man, all tattered and torn, that kissed the maiden, all forlorn.

Eula could see nothing but emergency flashers ahead and behind her. She could hear nothing but sirens and radio crackle and the whomp-whomp-whomp of rotor blades. And she thought of the dark thing to which she would soon give birth.

They linger.

She reached into her purse.

She looked at the children in the overhead mirror.

This will probably scar them for the rest of their lives.

But it can't be helped. And it won't be that messy. Not nearly as much mess as you would think.

BROKEN UP INSIDE

The sales clerk at the Sweetwater Reservoir Bait Shop gave Gaynell too much change back. The pack of Big Red gum cost eighty-five cents. Gaynell paid with a five, but the clerk must have thought it was a twenty, because he gave her back fifteen dollars too much.

Gaynell stood there at the register for a moment. Calculating. Not the dollars and cents (that much was obvious), but whether or not to speak up and say something. Tell the young cashier he'd made a mistake and hand him the money back.

Waiting in line behind her, there were two men dressed alike in sweat-stained John Deere caps and sleeveless Slayer t-shirts. Gaynell felt pressured to either speak up and say something, or step away so the two young men could make their purchase. They were carrying Styrofoam buckets with red nylon rope handles. She could see sluggish minnows in the murky bucket-water. They both looked at her with red-rimmed eyes, and their expressions seemed to say, *Do you have unfinished business?*

Gaynell decided she didn't have unfinished business,

tucked the money in her purse, and walked on out, gum in hand.

She sat in her white SUV for a minute and felt bad about herself. She had intended to spend her lunch break sitting in the sun on one of the granite slabs that encircled the manmade lake and enjoy her cinnamon gum while a cool breeze from the reservoir washed over her, but now she was upset and didn't know what to do. The clerk was a very young man with baby-fine blond hair and long, black, almost girlish eyelashes, and he would certainly have to make up for his register being short. From his own pocket, most likely.

By not speaking up, it was like she had stolen the money from him. Gaynell was a thief.

On the other hand, it was his mistake, not hers. She hadn't tricked him. Hadn't pulled some kind of switcheroo or distracted him with small talk. Paying the difference out of his own pocket would likely teach him a valuable lesson.

He might could have a baby at home and a wife pregnant with another one. That fifteen dollars might mean the difference between affording to buy formula for the baby and not being able to afford it. Gaynell very well could be taking food from the mouth of an infant.

Then of course, he could be a drug user who was just going to spend that money on more dope. Maybe those two men were there to buy marijuana from him. They had red eyes.

The right thing to do would be to give the money back. In her heart, she knew that.

When she was seventeen, Gaynell had hit a dog with her father's car. She had just been going to the store to get a Dr. Pepper and some gum (Teaberry back then, but she'd always been fond of chewing gum). Upset, she stopped the car and got out to check on the animal. The dog was whimpering, unable to move. Broken up inside. She knelt beside it and stroked it, watching red dust filter down onto the dirt road. It was just an old mutt. Mixed breed. Heinz 57 is what her father would have called it.

"You're going to be all right," she had said, trying to offer comfort. She wanted to help it. To save it. But it was only her second time driving alone by herself, and she knew that if her father found out that she had hit a dog with his car, he wouldn't trust her to drive it anymore. He didn't agree with girls driving, as it was.

So she left the dog on the side of the red dirt road and went on to the store. She was sure somebody would come along and help the animal. Or that there was nothing anybody could do to help it, and it would crawl off and die, alone and hidden. Or maybe it wasn't hurt as bad as it looked, and the dog would get up and go back to where it came from. So she left it.

On her way back from the store, Gaynell was chewing her gum and listening to the radio. The Eagles were singing "Hotel California," and she sang right along with them. She had put the incident with the dog out of her mind. The teenage brain worked well that way. Nonetheless, when she came up on the spot, she couldn't help but notice that the dog was still there on the side of the road. Her gum went sour in her mouth as she drove past. Nobody had stopped to help it. And it hadn't crawled off into the kudzu to die in private. Gaynell never chewed Teaberry gum ever again. Or listened to the Eagles.

Gaynell decided that she didn't want this fifteen dollars hanging over her head for the rest of her life. Or have to give up chewing Big Red. So she got out of the car and headed back to the bait shop. Outside the door, she was affronted by the bang of a gunshot and recoiled and crouched behind a metal garbage can. The two men came barreling out of the door and sped away in a primer-gray El Camino. The engine sounded deep and phlegmy like a prehistoric animal. Once it was long gone, she stood up and peeked through the bait shop window and saw the young clerk on the floor. There was a baseball bat a few inches from his hand, like he had come over the counter to stop those men.

Gaynell went on inside. The blood was pooling up underneath the boy. She could see a fine spray of it across his milky cheek and speckled in those long delicate eyelashes. Gaynell went to him, stepping over the gasping minnows that dotted the floor. The boy was whimpering. She knelt beside him.

"You're going to be all right," she said, and stroked his hair. "You're going to be all right."

Gaynell snapped open her purse, and before she left, she tucked the fifteen dollars into the boy's hand, and closed his fingers around it.

JOLENE

It was quiet in the bedroom. Mary Louise felt like she might cry. They had only been in bed for ten minutes and she knew it took Kent at least fifteen minutes to fall asleep.

So they both lay there, awake, in the dark.

She needed to say something to him. To clear the air. She had known about his infidelity for over a week now and finally made up her mind to get it out in the open.

Maybe infidelity wasn't the right word for it, but it was close enough.

All during dinner—taco salad—Mary Louise wanted to bring it up. And after the dishes were done, sitting on the couch watching *Wheel of Fortune* together, she almost said something. But didn't. Couldn't. She wanted to ask him about his cheating, but it was just too disturbing, too embarrassing. After the last puzzle was solved (CURIOSITY KILLED THE CAT BURGLAR), Kent went downstairs to the basement and worked on his model railroad. He had a whole little locomotive fantasy world constructed down there—mountains and valleys and Swiss villages and trestles and tunnels. Mary Louise stayed on the couch by herself and watched hour-long dramas about crime scene investigation.

Now, lying here beside him, she could smell vestiges of taco seasoning on his breath, as his exhalations evened out and deepened in the prelude to sleep.

"Kent?"

His breath caught in his throat, and he said, "Huh?"

She paused, quite dramatically, then said, "I just . . . I need to ask you something."

"What?"

"Do you still love me?"

She heard him sigh. Mary Louise knew that sigh well. She believed that all wives were familiar with that sigh. It was a sigh of resignation and exasperation. It was a sigh that said, *for Christ's sake, are you kidding me with this crap?* But she was surprised when his hand found her hand under the covers, squeezed it, and said, "Of course I do, honey."

"If there was somebody else, would you tell me?"

"There's nobody else. When would I have the time? Or the energy?"

"Kent, all I've ever wanted is for you to be happy. That's all I've ever wanted. And if I'm not what makes you happy, I just want you to—"

"Mary, I'm not cheating on you. I swear."

"I just want you to tell me. We'll work it out."

"There's nobody. I swear. I don't know what else to say."

"If there ever is, just tell me. Don't cheat on me. Don't humiliate me that way."

"You're the only woman in my life. I swear to God."

But that was a lie, and Mary Louise knew it. So she closed her eyes and let the hot tears flow in silence. And she thought, *Jolene. Jolene. Jolene. Jolene.* Over and over and over. Like a spell. An incantation. She pictured Jolene as she sent thoughts out to her, as though her rival were capable of hearing and responding.

Jolene, I'm begging of you, please don't take my man.

The week before, she'd gone down to the model train room. To clean. Kent didn't like her to clean down there. He was afraid she would break something or throw out some little piece worth keeping. But surfaces collected dust, and she didn't think a feather duster was going to destroy anything.

That particular day she had been a little bored. Kent had left the train out on the tracks. Usually he put it up. So Mary Louise flipped the power switch and heard the transformer hum to life. She nudged the switch forward just a little, and the locomotive moved ahead with hesitation. She pushed the switch a little more, and soon the nine-car train was making its way leisurely around the track. It went under a mountain, hooked a mailbag in a little town. It climbed to where Kent had set tracks high up along the walls with painted scenery. There was a cut-out near the ceiling, at the top edge of the drywall, painted to look like the bricked arch entrance to a tunnel. The HO scale train disappeared into the darkness behind the wall for a few seconds, and then reappeared from another cut-out.

It took about ninety seconds for the train to complete one circuit. She increased the speed, and it did it again, in just under a minute.

Really, it was pretty boring. Once she saw it complete the track, the novelty evaporated. There had been some small thrill in running it alone for the first time, but even that buzz had quickly dissipated. How on earth could a hobby like this keep anyone entertained for hours on end? My God, Kent spent entire weekends down here.

Mary Louise decided to try and see if she could get the train to complete the track in under forty-five seconds. That might be fun.

She had the thing flying pretty soon. She could smell the transformer heating up from pushing it so hard. She had it going so fast, that it derailed one time. She carefully picked the cars up, found no damage, aligned the grooved metal wheels back on the track, and decided to try one last time for the speed record.

The thing screamed down the track. Dangerous. Like an action movie. She imagined the train carrying a deadly virus or a nuclear bomb. If it derailed, it would mean the end of humanity. At this speed, every curve in the track was a potential disaster. She slowed it for the downhill mountain underpass, then barreled it through the little village, picking up considerable speed. It was the uphill climb to those elevated tracks near the ceiling that slowed her down, so she gave it full throttle. The transformer was hot to the touch and giving off the odor of burnt plastic. She was going to ease it back down once it got to the top but didn't time it right, and just as the train disappeared behind the drywall cut-out, she heard it jump the track and fall in the dark space behind the wall.

This was bad. In addition to the end of all humanity, if Kent found out Mary Louise had not only been playing with his train set, but had crashed it, he would be beyond upset.

The man was very particular about his model trains.

She carried a wooden bar stool over to the wall, climbed up, stuck her head through the tunnel opening and peered down into the empty space behind the drywall. It was too dark to see anything.

She went upstairs and found a little LED flashlight in the drawer under the microwave. While she was up there, she grabbed a pair of grill tongs from the utensil drawer, too, figuring she might be able to fish the train cars out from behind that wall.

Once Mary Louise was up on the stool, she stuck her head back through the cut-out. The opening was just barely wide enough for her fit her arm through, too. She clicked on the flashlight. And screamed.

She bumped the back of her head on the drywall, jerking away from the horror she saw back there. The shock and fear had caused her to recoil. She twisted and tumbled from the stool, landing face down on the repurposed ping pong table that supported the sprawling Alpine village.

She had seen a body behind the wall. A corpse.

Mary Louise lay on the table—miniature fir trees poking her stomach and breasts—and cried. She sobbed. She was married to a monster. A serial killer, maybe. She imagined herself doing the correct thing in this situation. She imagined herself getting up and calling 911 to report what she had found. Let the authorities sort it all out.

Fuck Kent.

That murdering motherfucker.

Then she remembered the cold snap last winter when she had been home alone because Kent was in Las Vegas at a human resources seminar. By herself in bed that night, she heard banging and cracking and called the police to report someone breaking in. A home invasion. Two deputies showed up and cleared the house. They explained that there was no sign of forced entry, and that the sounds were caused by the house contracting in the extreme cold. It was their third such call that night. They had been nice enough about it, but Mary Louise saw the two men exchange a wink and a grin on their way out.

She'd felt like a damn fool.

Maybe she should make sure. Before she called the police. Wouldn't there be a smell? If there was a body back there? It would stink, wouldn't it? She should look one last time. So she could be for-sure. So she wouldn't make a fool of herself. Again.

Flashlight in hand, Mary Louise climbed back up the stool and peered into the recess. It was a body, alright. No doubt about it. A woman's body. But there was something odd about it. For one thing, the body was sitting up. At a little table. With tea cups set out. Tea for two. The woman had auburn hair. Her arms were resting on the tiny table. And there was just something about it that was so familiar. And then it came to Mary Louise that she had set her dolls up like that when she was a little girl, and what she was looking at was not a dead body at all, but a doll. A life size play-pretty.

Kent must have set this up as a practical joke to pull on his buddies. Except that didn't make sense, because Kent didn't ever have friends over. Not down here, anyway. He was particular about people being around his trains.

Mary Louise took the barbecue tongs, reached down, and prodded the doll. It slumped over and fell to the floor—on top of the derailed train.

How on earth was she going to get down there and get those cars? It wasn't possible. She pulled her head out of the wall and looked around the room, trying to come up with an idea. Maybe she could hook the train out with a fishing pole. Or make something out of coat hangers. She scanned the room. From up on the stool, Mary Louise could see on top of the supply case that rested against the wall just to the left of the tunnel cut-out. The shelves were loaded with supplies like pails of plaster of Paris and extra track and transformers and things like that. Cans of spray paint—green for foliage, white for snow, brown for rocks. From where she stood on the stool, she could see that the top of the shelving unit was covered in thick dust, and even as she reminded herself to run a feather duster up there, she noted that there was a clean spot along the corner. A clean spot in the shape of three fingers and a thumb. As though somebody put their hand up there regularly.

Mary Louse climbed down from the stool and reached up to that spot on the shelf. She used her hip for leverage and gave it a good push. The whole unit moved easily. It seemed to float over the carpeted floor like it was on casters.

There was a door behind it. Just a plain plywood rectangle with a little hook-and-eye latch. It shouldn't have bothered her, this little plain door.

But it did.

Mary opened the door. A long narrow area back there ran the entire length of the wall. Narrow, yes, but roomy enough. Back behind the doll and the little card table, there was a single-size mattress on the floor.

It had clean sheets on it.

She pulled the doll out into the main room. It was heavy, but not as heavy as a real person. Maybe seventy pounds. Dressed casual in blue jeans and a t-shirt.

She was beautiful. The doll. The doll was beautiful. Out in the light, the auburn hair was like flame. The latex skin made Mary think of pink-tinged ivory. The eyes were brilliant emeralds, piercing, drawing Mary Louise in. She couldn't look away. The doll was beautiful.

If she hadn't seen the mattress, Mary Louise's next thought would never have entered her mind. It was too bizarre. It was beyond her comprehension. She could believe Kent was infatuated with the doll, that he was some kind of closet sissy enthralled by huge dolls. But the idea that he kept this doll in order to have sexual relations with it? Not possible. But she had to know. So Mary Louise undressed the doll.

It wasn't a cheap blow-up novelty toy with a circular open mouth like she had seen in comedy movies. It was just like a real person. A replica. Another woman.

It had full, perfectly formed breasts. And down below, what appeared to be a functioning, anatomically correct vagina. Most disturbing, Mary Louise noted that the pink flushed skin tone around the lips was flaking. Worn away. Kent had been getting plenty of use out of it.

That sick son of a bitch.

When she lifted the doll's leg to put the jeans back on, Mary Louise saw that there was a word embossed on the sole of the foot. JOLENE. And under that, a model number.

She searched the little secret room some more and found an envelope. It held a receipt.

Silicone Fantasy Doll.

Model: Jolene.

Weight 30 Kg.

Hair: Auburn

Eyes: Emerald Green

7" Mouth Cavity

Real Human Hair

The total price made her stomach ache. Mary Louise had been doing the dishes by hand for over a year, because Kent said they couldn't afford to replace the broken dishwasher. She put the invoice down after reading there was an option to purchase extra faces for the doll, and that it came with inserts for "hygiene and easy clean-up."

It took her the rest of the afternoon to put the train room (and the sex doll room) back to rights. She had to replace three fir trees that she'd crushed when she landed on the table. But she thought everything would pass inspection.

Then Mary Louise went upstairs, took a Xanax, and lay down on the couch.

What was she going to do? What was she going to do about Kent? About that doll?

Jolene.

She finally got up the nerve to ask Kent if he was cheating on her, but he lied and swore he wasn't. In the end, she decided to do nothing. Not to confront Kent any further. Not yet. She wanted to come to terms with this herself before she dared peer into her husband's sick mind.

Mary Louise stewed on it. Came to view the doll as a rival. Competition. Thought about buying green contacts and dyeing her hair red.

During the day, she couldn't rest knowing that thing was down there. In her house. Under her roof. She decided she wanted to look at it again. So she went downstairs and pulled Jolene out of the dark. Mary Louise noticed that the sheet on the mattress back there was a different color now. He'd changed it.

She carried Jolene upstairs and sat her on the couch.

"Want a Coke?" She asked it. "Slice of pie, maybe? How about an EPT pregnancy test?"

Mary Louise fixed herself a cup of hazelnut coffee and turned on the TV. From the loveseat, she sipped her coffee and watched *The View*. Jolene sat across from her, on the couch, looking toward a plastic ficus tree. Mary Louise got up and tilted the doll's head so that it was watching the television.

After a while, Mary Louise said, "I know you're screwing him."

Jolene neither confirmed nor denied the accusation, and a little later, Mary Louise took Jolene back downstairs and finished up her housework.

She got in the habit of bringing Jolene upstairs every day and putting her back downstairs before Kent got home. She knew it was a weird thing to do, but she liked having the doll visible. Where she could keep an eye on it. Not hidden away.

Not an unseen threat.

Mary Louise would sit and watch television with Jolene. She would do her housework and drift in and out of the living room. Talking to the doll about anything that popped into her mind.

"Did you ever see that movie, Harper Valley PTA? *With Barbara Eden? That was based on a song. Do you remember that song called "Ode to Billy Joe?" What do you think they were throwing off that bridge?"*

"We were best friends. Talked all the time. Cut-up with each other. Laughed. We haven't laughed together in years."

"He's a stranger to us now. Our only son. A stranger. Maybe you blame the drugs. Maybe he was just born like that. I don't know. Maybe we did something that broke him inside. The way we brought him up. I just don't know."

"No, I was a teacher's aide for a long time. Taught deaf children. I still remember a lot of the signs. If you want, I can show you some. Look, this is "water." Three fingers like a W. Tap 'em against your chin. See? This one means "bathroom." And this is "friend." Like this. Let me see your hands. Hook your fingers together. That's it. Friend."

"And he looks me right in the eye, and he says, 'actually, I do still want sex. Just not from you.'"

"And now I'm just a housewife. That's the right word for it, too. I'm married to this house."

"I prayed about it. That's all you can do."

"We were just teenagers. He put an anonymous love letter in my parent's mailbox. My daddy opened it."

"It was atypical. Precancerous. So I was okay. Thank God."

"Mr. Elway, the principal, wanted to have an affair with me. He made it plain."

"Love is an illusion for young people. That's what I've decided."

At some point, and without her realizing that a line had been crossed, Jolene began responding to Mary Louise. She wasn't crazy. She understood that Jolene wasn't really speaking, that it was her own voice she was hearing. But if someone had snuck up to the living room window to spy, they would have seen Mary Louise talking to a life-size doll, hands gesticulating—wishing for one of the cigarettes they hadn't held in over a decade. And in the silence that followed, the peeping tom would have seen Mary Louise cock her head to the side, listening to a high-pitched feminine voice that only she could hear.

It took them a long time to work up to the one thing that they each really wanted to know. *What was he like? What was Kent like when he was alone with you?* And so they told each other. Voices hesitant at first. It was uncomfortable. But the truth was gotten at. And they each made peace with it.

And with that peace, Mary Louise felt no humiliation when she acknowledged that Jolene had bested her. She pleaded with her not to take her man. Jolene could have her choice of men, but Mary Louise could never love again. She begged, knowing that her happiness depended on whatever Jolene decided to do. She put it in Jolene's hands. That was all she could do.

As Mary Louise was taking Jolene downstairs before Kent got home, she paused before opening the secret door, and asked Jolene if Kent had ever taken the time to show her his train set, or did he just throw her on the mattress and pump on her? The train was most important thing in his life, after all. It trumped both his women. So she decided to take a minute and show it to her before she put her up for the day.

She pointed out the river pass, the woodland scenes, the coal loader, the functional crossing gates. All of it.

She got the locomotive moving, too. The throttle on the transformer went from zero (stop) to 100 (full.) By the time she got it up to eighty, the transformer was getting warm. Mary Louise knew she was showing off for Jolene, and pushed it up to ninety. The train shook and shimmied and rocketed down the track. The power pack got hot to the touch, and gave off an ozone odor. The train was whipping along the tracks like death on steel wheels.

Mary Louise pushed the throttle up to ninety-five, cutting her eyes to Jolene and giggling. It was at that moment that two things happened simultaneously. They were both things Mary Louise should have foreseen. First, the train derailed. And then the low rumbling of the electric garage door opener could be heard—even downstairs.

The train was half on and half off the track. Wrecked. It needed to be righted. Jolene was sitting in a cane-back chair, staring mutely at the calamity. She needed to be put away. And the garage door was already closing.

When Kent came inside the house, he would look for Mary Louise. Often, if he'd had a bad day, he grabbed a Coke from the fridge and headed straight for the basement.

There simply wasn't time to put Jolene away and fix the train both. So she left everything as it was and ran upstairs to intercept Kent.

Her decision to run out of the basement like that would damn their already ruined lives.

But even if Mary Louise had noticed that the derailment left the metal train wheels touching both the center rail and the outside rail, she would have thought nothing of it. She would not have known that it could cause a short circuit in the electricity that ran through the track and powered the locomotive's engine. And she certainly had no way of knowing that this short circuit would draw excessive current from the maxed-out transformer, or that the circuit breaker built into the transformer was faulty, that it would fail.

Upstairs, Mary Louise threw her arms around Kent, told him she loved him, and said she wanted to go out for dinner. Golden Corral. Kent said no, he was tired. But Mary Louise pouted and cajoled and produced a few tears until he finally relented. He didn't want a repeat of the *do you still love me?* discussion.

Over dinner, Mary Louise decided that there was nothing to do but to let Kent find out that she knew everything. Let him walk downstairs when they got home and see for himself that his secret was out. That she knew about Jolene. She found peace in this. It was time. And there was a possibility that the shared knowledge could bring them closer together. That there could be a healing. And with this hope in mind, she tried to talk to her husband. Just little things. To reconnect with him. To be authentic. To be his friend.

"Did you know this means water?"

"Do you remember when I had that mole removed?"

"I was thinking about calling Ben. See how he is."

"Remember when my daddy read that letter you sent me?"

"Maybe I can give you a massage tonight?"

"Kent, Kent, you never listen to me. What are thinking about?"

"I'm sorry. I just want to get home. I have an idea for a new route."

And Mary Louise thought, *fine*. They would go home. And he would see Jolene sitting out in the open, gazing at the train disaster. Like a lone survivor. And then Kent would know.

They didn't talk on the drive back. With the windows rolled up, the inside of the car was a silent vacuum. And when they turned onto their street and saw the red staccato lights of the fire trucks, Mary Louise remembered the transformer. How hot it got. The ozone smell.

Their home was fully ablaze. They got out of the car and ran to it. The firefighters kept them back. The heat was an enormous wall.

Mary Louise imagined Jolene, the flames licking her silicone skin, the ivory flesh blistering and popping and charring. The real-human-hair singing. The eyes of emerald green going dark. All of Jolene reduced to a liquid pool, bubbling blackly away to nothingness.

Kent was telling her something, his voice rising over the chant of the flames, but Mary Louise was having trouble understanding. She thought he might have said something about his trains. But she couldn't hear him. What she heard was Jolene's feminine high-pitched cries, reedy and sharp with pain and terror. Calling out to Mary Louise in a voice that broke her heart. A voice that was all the more haunting because it was her own.

Kent was shouting now, trying to get Mary Louise's attention. She focused on him and heard, ". . . fingers. What are you doing?"

She looked down and saw that she had thrust her arms out in front of herself, holding them stiff and rigid in a way that made her think about zombies in old-time monster movies, but she had her forefingers hooked together, forming a symbol, like something religious. And she said, "Friend. It means friend."

Mary Louise looked up at her husband, searching his face for acceptance—or at least understanding—but what she saw was that the red light from the emergency beacons and the yellow flickering of the flames had colored Kent's face in way that made him look like a villager. A tribesman. And she understood that she and Kent were—in this exact moment—as close as they would ever be. Homeless primitives stripped of all artifice. Their primordial selves. Things might be better for a little while, but she knew in her heart that from this moment forward, they would begin filling their lives again. A new house would be secured, complete with carpeted man cave. Mary Louise's Xanax prescription would get refilled—the dosage likely increased. Maybe Kent wouldn't feel like starting from scratch with his model railroad hobby. But something else would take its place.

And maybe her husband would have need of her one cold night.

But before long, something else would take her place.

YOUR WORST WEEK
STARTS NOW

The online post said, "Since you have read this, you will be told good news today. If you don't repost this, your worst week starts now."

Goddamnit.

Jared cursed himself for having glanced at the meme. He enjoyed a good aphorism, a spurious Einstein quote, or even a cute lolcat as much as the next guy. But—*Goddamnit*—he hated the ones that relied on emotional or spiritual blackmail to replicate themselves.

If you don't repost this, your worst week starts now.

He usually scanned these things to look for keywords like *Jesus* or *luck* or *sick child*—and scrolled past those before the message could be logged into his brain. Like a pathogen. But whoever created this one was pretty smart.

Since you have read this. As soon as your eyes touched those words, you were complicit. There was no escape. The deed was done, the snare tripped.

It was perhaps a finer opening line than *Call me Ishmael.*

Jared knew he should just keep scrolling and try to

forget those words. But he also knew that if he did that, he would have a shadow hanging over him for the rest of his day. Wondering. Worried.

But he couldn't repost it, either. His friends would think he was stupid. A superstitious fool.

Even worse, he didn't want to burden anybody he knew with a dilemma like this.

The post was a threat, pure and simple.

He had to transfer this burden to another person. A stranger. But how?

Jared printed the message and put it in his pocket. It didn't say it had to be posted online.

On his way to work, he stopped at Egleston Children's Hospital and took an elevator to the Childhood Cancer and Blood Disorder Clinic. Sure enough, there was a bulletin board right there in the vestibule next to the elevator. The board was covered in thumbtacked notices—folks offering in-home services, looking for rideshares, forming support groups. Jared yanked out the tacks and put them in his pocket until the board was completely bare. Naked cork. He tossed the scraps of paper into the trash can.

He unfolded the meme and placed it squarely in the middle of the denuded board. He pushed a pin into the top left corner of the paper, another in the top right corner, and a final tack he placed bottom center. A trinity.

Unburdened, Jared seemed to float back down to the parking deck. When he reached into his pocket for his car keys, the thumbtacks were still in there, and he impaled his thumb on one of them. The sharp metal tip went under the nail, deep into the nail bed.

He stood next to his car for a few minutes, sucking the blood from his thumb and thinking about what sort of pathogens might have been lurking on that tack.

After a wonderful appointment with their son's oncologist, the Ellison's were in grand spirits as they approached the vestibule of the cancer clinic. Mr. and Mrs. Ellison both reckoned there was likely no more profoundly beautiful a word in the English language than *remission.* Good things were finally starting to happen for them. They let go of their son's hand so he could have the small thrill of pushing the button to call up the elevator.

While they waited, the bulletin board caught Mrs. Ellison's eye. Her hand went unconsciously to the gold crucifix around her neck as she read what was posted there.

"Since you have read this, you will be told good news today. If you don't repost this, your worst week starts now."

Ensnared, she removed the pins.

REGULAR, NORMAL PEOPLE

Religion is a funny thing. We've all got a little bit of it inside us. Even if you say you don't believe in God or Jesus or Zeus or Pan. There are no atheists in foxholes. That's a very true statement. If your child is in ICU after getting run over by a car, or you're waiting for the biopsy results from the lump on your left testicle, or you're hunkered down in your basement while a tornado barrels right through the middle of your neighborhood—you pray. If you believe in God and Jesus, then you direct your prayers straight to them. If you've maybe fallen away from Christianity and have started thinking Jesus is just a made-up story, well, when the shit hits the fan—or when the tumor hits your balls—you're gonna revert right back to believing. You're going to grasp at straws. And if you're maybe one of those people who never believed in a damn thing, never believed in anything supernatural at all, well, when the doctors tell you that your little boy might end up brain dead if they can't get the intracranial pressure to go down, then I submit that you will fall to your knees and pray and beg and beseech whatever power might be out there to please, please, please intervene and save your child.

There are no atheists in foxholes. Everybody believes (or at least hopes) in something beyond themselves when they're alone in the dark with no chance to escape.

We are regular, normal people. We live in the suburbs. There is nothing special about us.

I guess me and Jennie were about on the same page religion-wise when we got married. Christians. That's the way we both were raised, but we didn't go to church much (at all) or even say grace before meals. But we believed, more or less. Neither one of us wanted to go to Hell. We accepted that Jesus Christ was the path to heaven.

I understand now why cultures frown on people from different religions getting married. When you're young and in love, that stuff seems insignificant. But when you're older and not-as-in-love, and you can see death as a real eventuality, your life moves in a more spiritual direction. That's when those differences can start to show, to put a strain on a marriage. That's the way it was with me and Jennie. She started believing more and more, and I started believing less and less.

It's like echoes that get stronger instead of weaker. When we first got married, I only drank on the weekends. Maybe a six pack on Friday and Saturday night. Then pretty soon I started wanting a beer or two after I got home from Overstock World on weeknights, to unwind. It just got to be more and more, and after a while, I switched to vodka because it was a lot cheaper than beer. More bang for your buck. Vodka and grapefruit juice. That's what I drank seven nights a week. I'd sit up late at night and play Spades on the computer with other people online and my Internet name that I gave myself was *Vodkaniac.*

Do you see the echo? How it got stronger? How I started out just having some beer on the weekends and ended up as Vodkaniac as the echo got stronger? That's like what happened with Jennie and the religion stuff.

A girlfriend invited her to church one Sunday. And she liked it well enough I guess. A social thing more than anything else.

Then it just got to be more and more. Like how I was drinking more and more.

She started saying grace over our meals. Which was nice. That reminded me of being a kid and how my father always mumbled a little something up to God before we ate the dinner my mother had prepared.

But it got where she would say weird things, too. Like if we got in an argument about me drinking too much, she would say, "I plead the blood of the lamb," and just walk away. I didn't even know what that meant. Still don't.

If anything good happened, she would say God had made it happen. Like if we were real far behind on the bills, close to getting our electricity shut off or something, and I worked two extra overnight shifts and brought home a check that was fat with overtime, she would say, God had really blessed us.

I would say, no, he did not. I blessed us. I'm the one who put in all those hours under fluorescent lights, setting up endcaps and in-store displays. She would say that

God took care of all our needs, and He made that overtime available and kept me healthy enough to work it. That she had prayed and asked Him to get all our bills paid, and He had answered her prayers.

That made me really mad. For one thing, it just completely took my free will out of the equation, like I was just some kind of zombie being controlled by God. So even though I did all the work, God got all the credit. Jennie got some credit too, because she was the one who had prayed and asked God to provide for our needs. I did all the work, and God and Jennie took all the credit.

She started at a new church. Fundamentalist. Charismatic. It was called Church of God of Prophecy, and it plain scared me. She drug me in there one time. The preacher got up on stage and started talking in tongues. It was just gibberish. It wasn't any language; it was just something he was making up on the spot. He walked back and forth, holding his belly and laughing. It wasn't like real laughing, he was going, "Ha! Ha! Ha!—Ha! Ha! Ha!" over and over again. Jennie knew I was greatly disturbed. She leaned over and told me he was "laughing in the spirit." Said it was joy that was supernaturally given.

Those people weren't but one step away from snake handling, and I didn't want a goddamn thing to do with them.

It seemed like the harder she believed, the more I questioned it.

There was a bad tornado up in Alabama, ripped right through a residential neighborhood. All the houses on one side of the street were completely destroyed, flattened like a giant had stepped on them. On the other side of the street, all the houses were fine, not even a loose shutter or shingle blown off the roof. It was just one of those freakish weather things you hear about sometimes. We watched while they interviewed the people on CNN, and this woman whose house was spared talked about how it sounded like a freight train tearing through the neighborhood. She said her house was groaning and shaking, and they were all hunkered down in the basement, and just praying, praying to God to save them, to spare her and her family.

And He did. Their home stood through the storm. Not a speck of damage.

Jennie turned to me and said that proved the existence of God. If you worshiped Him and acknowledged Him, then He would acknowledge you in your time of need. But if you turned your back on Him, then He would turn His back on you.

And all I could think was, well what about all them people on the other side of the street? They weren't praying? None of them believed in God? That was just crazy. But I didn't speak up, because I'd learned to keep my mouth shut. No matter what kind of logic I tried to use, there was always a reason, even if that reason was *we'll never understand the mind of God.*

One time, I told her I just didn't understand the concept of hell. That if I had a child, and I needed to punish that child, I wouldn't shove him in a furnace and burn him to death for ten million years. Why would God do that to us if we were his children? It just didn't make sense.

Jennie said I was beset by demons that were clouding my mind, and she started in on how God had sacrificed his only begotten son, so that we could have forgiveness and cleansing of our sins. It was my choice to turn my back on salvation when Jesus had showed me the way. But you know, that still didn't answer my question about a parent shoving his child in a furnace. Sounded to me like God was one evil motherfucker.

She had this mole on her thigh, and it started looking weird. The mole was kind of bubbly, like road tar on a hot day. She didn't want to go to the doctor, said she would pray for divine healing. I said okay, but I went to the computer and looked up skin cancer on the Internet. Looked at pictures. There wasn't any doubt in my mind that the mole on Jennie's thigh was cancer. Melanoma. And melanoma is the worst kind of skin cancer you can get. It spreads.

I told her what I found out. That I was pretty sure she had melanoma, but she said God was going to heal her, He was going to deliver her of it. I told her that I didn't think that was the way God worked. I said, if you're standing on train tracks, and a train is coming straight at you, you don't close your eyes and ask God to make the train disappear. You step off the tracks. And if you've got cancer on your thigh, you don't pray it away; you go to the fucking doctor.

She wouldn't do it. I started getting myself used to the idea of living as a widower, because I knew that's how this was all going to end up. But do you know what happened? That spot on her thigh just kind of started drying up. It turned brownish red and got real flaky and powdery. And then, after about a week, it scabbed over and fell off. Like it was never there. Now, you tell me, did God do that? I sure don't know. Maybe He did.

Jennie ended up getting pregnant. Which was kind of a miracle in itself, because we didn't hardly ever have sex anymore, mostly because I was usually too drunk to perform in that capacity. Sometimes I think me and Jennie both have a hole inside of us, and I'm trying to fill my hole up with alcohol, and she's trying to fill hers up with God. What neither one of us knew was that hole can't ever be filled up.

When we found out she was expecting, I did slow down on my drinking, and Jennie pulled back on her religion. I wanted to be a good father. We had been trying to have a family for a long time, but Jennie just couldn't ever get pregnant. We're just normal, regular people, so we didn't have money to pay for fertility treatments or artificial insemination or anything like that. Time went by and we kind of gave up trying; I started drinking and she started testifying. I guess probably not having a child was a big part of that hole we were trying to fill up.

So of course she said God had answered her prayers and knocked her up, but I could notice a kind of calming of the religious mania, and I'm sure she noticed I switched from vodka back to beer. Things seemed like they were getting better for us. The echoes were dying out instead of getting stronger.

Jennie looked like someone had planted a watermelon seed in her belly and it grew. She was beautiful.

There were some problems with the pregnancy. She got gestational diabetes and I had to give her insulin shots or else the baby would get too big inside her. That got her scared that she might lose the baby or it would end up being born retarded or something. She turned to The Lord for help and got back in with that church.

They held a healing service for her. I went. How could I not go? It was my wife and my baby.

The congregation all prayed for her while the preacher brought her up to the little pulpit, laid hands on her and commanded the demon that had sickened her womb and threatened her child to be expelled in the name and the everlasting power of the living God, Jesus Christ. Then he got down on his knees and started that laughing in the spirit. "Ha! Ha! Ha!—Ha! Ha! Ha!" Over and over again right into Jennie's privates. I thought about my little unborn child in there feeling those sound waves washing over it.

The preacher reached under the podium and brought out a plain pine box with a screen lid. He opened it up and brought out two snakes, looked like copperheads to me. At first I thought he was going to put one on Jennie, but she was already walking back to our pew. The preacher held the snakes up over his head, and let them crawl up his arm, over his shoulders and around his neck. He would pick one off his body, and let it crawl back up his arm again, all the time just bellowing how this church was filled with the loving spirit of the lord

Jesus Christ, and how his belief in the Lord would keep the poisonous serpents from biting him.

I wanted a drink.

Since I had gone to the church with her, Jennie agreed to keep going to the doctor, too. That's what marriage is. Compromise. She said that she had been divinely delivered and given a supernatural healing. She knew that the baby was fine, but she would go back to the doctor for me, for my peace of mind.

After her last appointment, she said the doctor told her that they couldn't detect a fetal heartbeat. They did an ultrasound and that confirmed it. The baby had died inside of her. They told her that they could put her in the hospital and chemically induce labor, or she could continue to carry it and let it come out naturally on its own. She would give birth to a dead baby.

The news shook me up pretty bad. I knew if it was me, I'd go to the hospital and let them get it out of me. I couldn't walk around day after day knowing I was carrying a dead child inside of me. I didn't even know if I could stand to stay in the house with her, knowing she had that dead thing in her womb. It broke my heart. I told her she should let them take it out.

She had this wild look in her eyes and laughed at me the way an adult laughs at a child who says something naïve and cute. She said those tests didn't confirm anything. That they were wrong, and if somehow they were right, that her child really had died inside her, then God would bring her baby back to life.

We waited to see if God was going to bless us with a

miracle and our baby was going to be born happy and healthy, or if Jennie would spontaneously abort the poor dead thing.

I set up camp on the couch. I couldn't sleep in the bedroom with her. I'm sorry, but I couldn't. She was on her own.

The preacher from the Church of God of Prophecy made a housecall. He stayed in there with her for three hours, and I could hear him speaking in tongues. I could hear that Santa Claus chortle. Laughing in the spirit. After he left, I looked in on her, and I saw in the corner that the preacher had left his pine box behind. The one with the screen top. To let in air.

The baby came in the night. It was born dead just like the doctor said. She won't let me take it away from her, said Jesus was going to heal our child, and that I had demons in me, and that I had to rebuke those demons so that our child could live.

At some point, I'm going to have to call somebody to come get her out of there. The fire department, maybe. I don't know.

We are regular, normal people. You need to understand that. We live in the suburbs. There is nothing special about us.

She's in there now—with those copperheads crawling all over her, holding our dead baby, and laughing in the spirit.

I'm gonna go out and get me a bottle of vodka. And pray.

STARLIGHT PEPPERMINT
(NSFW II)

I remember the first time I saw you. I was in my car—drive-thru banking—to get a check cashed. And even though I was on the far outside lane, you looked across all five traffic aisles and made eye contact with me. Yes, the security camera captured my image, and I'm sure it was on a monitor right there next to you, but you crossed time and space, to meet my eyes with yours. And when my money arrived through the pneumatic tube, I found you'd slipped a piece of candy into the envelope.

Starlight peppermint.

I wondered if you did that on purpose. If you were sending me a message.

I remember, too, later that August, it was hot and humid. The air conditioner in my car didn't work—and I'll never forget this—I was making a withdrawal. You greeted me by name. And when the clear plastic canister came through the tube, I grabbed it and held it in my lap while I twisted open the top. It was the oddest sensation. Icy vapor from inside the air-conditioned bank flowed out of the canister and pooled into my lap. I lifted the container to my face, and the cold dry air spilled from it, brushing my lips and nose. I could smell you. Your perfume. It was like standing next to you. It was like you sent the essence of yourself through time and space, just to get to me. I was so affected that I couldn't even speak. I replaced the canister and sped away. I hope I didn't hurt your feelings.

Driving home, I wondered if you did that on purpose. If you sent that little bit of you, to me, on purpose.

Two days later, I was back with a deposit. I drove around the bank first, scouting it out, so I would know which lane was yours. This time I had a plan. I was so nervous, I couldn't bring myself to speak or look at you. I wanted to appear distracted, so I turned up the radio and snapped my fingers and bobbed my head and waited for you to send me the receipt for my deposit. And when the transport canister slid down the tube and landed, I grabbed it and drove off. I kept the canister and drove away.

I had your air. Your perfumed essence, trapped in the plastic cylinder. Like a genie in a bottle. I had you.

I figured this must be a common-enough occurrence in drive-thru banking. People accidentally taking the tube container. I even searched online for the words *bank drove off with canister,* and there were over twelve million results. It happens all the time. Most likely by distracted people listening to the radio.

That night, I put you in my bed. The canister you. I laid you in the clean sheets while I took a shower. I wanted to be fresh. And then I fixed us two glasses of wine, to reduce anxiety, so we could be ourselves with each other.

I opened you. Consumed you. It was heaven. I know you felt it too.

The next day, I went inside the bank, and I asked for you by name—for Laurie. Because of course I've seen your gold-plastic name tag. The inside-teller (Roberta) told me you were busy and that she would be happy to help me, but I stood off to the side and waited for you. When you finally came out and saw me, you had this funny look on your face, almost like you didn't recognize me. I smiled at you—sheepish, embarrassed, guilty. And I held up the canister. I said I was sorry. Understanding broke across your face, and you grinned and cocked your head to the side and asked me if I did it on purpose. Ha-ha. Then you laughed some more and said don't worry, it happens all the time. It felt like you were reading my mind. Like you were sending me a message. Then I watched you open the canister. It was just a reflex on your part. Like maybe you were a little bit nervous and didn't know what to do with your hands. I watched your fingers slip inside, and I thought about the residue from last night that was in there, coating the circular walls, and how my essence was on your fingers now, and how later, you might put your fingers to your lips and part of me would be inside of you.

In a rushing breath, I told you how good of a job you were doing at the bank, and how courteous and professional you always were to me, and how you made me feel like my business was truly appreciated, and that I wanted to tell your manager what an asset you are to the bank, but I was late for an appointment and if you would just give me your business card, I could call the manager later and tell him exactly who I was complimenting.

So you gave me your card.

Laurie Ciresi.

Customer Service Specialist.

Ciresi is not a common name. Not common at all. You were easy to track down. But you knew that would be the case, didn't you?

Many nights, I watch from the stand of weeping willows behind your house. Sometimes with binoculars, and sometimes I just go right up and look in. You should really cut those hedges. They are a security risk. Or get your husband to do it. I don't think he's right for you. You two almost never sleep together. That says a lot.

Now that the weather is getting crisp, sometimes you open your windows to let in the evening air. When I get up close, I can smell your essence seeping out. It reminds me of how we first met, at your work, and how you sent me the air you breathe through the pneumatic tube. How I wondered if you did that on purpose. Ha-ha. It makes me smile now. How I brought the canister home, and then brought it back to you with a little bit of me left inside. Molecules of me. And now here I am, waiting for you, out under the stars. *Starlight*, remember? I wonder how many billions of years our atoms have swirled around the universe, only to arrive here, tonight, to be at this moment, bathed in starlight.

Time and space converge like the cards of a shuffled deck, and here we are.

What happens next?

I notice that you forgot to close your bedroom window all the way tonight. I can't help but wonder if you did that on purpose. If you are sending me a message.

I surely do wonder.

WICHITA LINEMAN

I looked away from her, to where the kitchen floor used to be.

"But we already have plenty of cookie sheets," I said.

I was careful to keep my tone neutral when I said it, but the very act of reaching for that note of neutrality gave my speaking voice a stilted gait, like a drunk trying too hard not to slur his words. No. I'll tell you what it sounded like. What I sounded like. I sounded like an actor in a play. Like I was on a stage in some crummy community theatre somewhere.

I have this dream sometimes, a nightmare, where I'm about to start work, and someone makes me smoke a marijuana cigarette right before I climb the utility pole, and when I get up there, I realize the joint had been dipped in formaldehyde or laced with PCP or something. And then I'm falling from the sky. From the lines. That's how this felt. Unreal.

Our cat peeked out of an old Pennzoil carton and watched us with copper yellow eyes. Waiting to see what would happen. Even it could sense the tension between us.

She looked down at the cookie sheet, her lips a tight

crease. Like her mouth was a piece of folded notebook paper. I watched the kitty jump out of the box and take off for parts unknown. I run across dead cats fairly often in my line of work.

"Don't you want it?" she said.

"Of course I want it. It's nice." Neutral. Maybe just a hair stilted.

"It's nonstick. See? That new diamond-dust stuff. Expensive. And I got it for less than a dollar."

"It's really nice. It's just that we have like seventeen sheet pans already. I don't think we can fit anymore under the stove."

"We can keep it inside the oven and take it out whenever we want to cook."

"Maybe we should just throw away a couple of the old ones."

That didn't go over so well. Even today, I still see her dark eyes glowing. The crease deepened. Severe. It had been bad between us for a long time now.

"No," she said. "You never know when you might need that many cookie sheets. What about at Christmas when you roll out all those sausage balls? You could use the old cookie sheets to make the sausage balls ahead of time and store them in the refrigerator until you're ready to cook. See?"

She had me there. In the unlikely event that I catered a holiday party and needed to serve about seven hundred sausage-and-cheese balls, I would truly have need for all those pans. I'm not a caterer. I am a lineman for the county.

"Well, it sure is a nice one," I said, and wedged the diamond-dusted sheet pan into the metal drawer under the stove. I would be goddamned if I was going to start storing pans in the oven. That's where we kept the groceries.

Diamond dust. Stardust. Billion year old carbon. God help me.

I didn't want to be standing there talking about cookie sheets. I was on call that night and already worried about the weather. I really don't mind the rain, but ice and sleet are hard on the lines. And if it snowed, that stretch down south wouldn't ever stand the strain. Wet snow causes trees to fall, limbs to break, and it can build up on the lines. Eventually the weight of it will make them snap. Time. Pressure. Accumulation.

It was the same way with me and her. It started gradual. Little by little. So little I didn't even notice it happening. I don't think she noticed it either. There was no intent on her part. I don't blame her. I can honestly say I don't blame her.

She started off by collecting the pull tabs off cans of Coke and Pepsi and any kind of soda pop. This was a long time ago. There was something on the Internet about Bill Gates would pay a nickel for every pull tab you collected. I forget why exactly. It was never true anyway. Just one of those things you would see on the Internet back when it was new and people would believe anything they read there. Emails that had been forwarded about a million times, full of those little chevron marks.

Pretty soon she had jars and buckets full of those pull tabs. Kind of pretty, actually. Big chunks of glitter. She was still a school teacher back then. Third grade. So she had all these little kids bringing in pull tabs from home. One little girl cut her finger pretty bad pulling one off, and the principal finally told my wife to stop before someone got sued. The bad part was that the little girl's finger ended up getting infected. That flesh eating bacteria. It was bad. To save her life, they had to take the girl's arm off at the shoulder. The court awarded the family three million dollars from the school district.

We had big cafeteria-size pickle jars full of those pull tabs in the cabinets and under the bathroom sink, buckets of them sitting out on the counters and tucked away in corners here and there. I mentioned how pretty they were. I used to run my fingers through them, scoop them up in handfuls and sprinkle them back in. I used to want to take a bucket of them to work with me. On a good clear day. And get good and high up there among those humming lines, feel the whine in my head, in my teeth, and just toss a bucketful of those pull tabs up to the blue sky, up to God, and watch them rain down like diamonds in the sun. I never did that, though. The thought of that little girl's blood maybe mixed in there with all that glitter and glam.

That was when I was still drinking. I was more inclined to fanciful thoughts. Diamonds. I heard once that diamonds were made out of carbon plus two other ingredients: Pressure. And time.

We're all made out of carbon. That's all we are.

Carbon. What do we become when you add pressure and time?

After a while, everybody got a little wiser about the Internet, and she finally came to understand that Bill Gates was not going to pay her five cents for every one of those pull tabs. I can tell you this much though: if he had, we would have been by-God rich.

All of that was a long time ago. Time is a funny thing. It tricks you. From where I'm at now, time has lost its meaning. If it ever had any. Diamonds, remember? What I'm saying is that by the time you read this, Bill Gates could be long dead. He could be floating around out there in the stars with Steve Jobs and Alexander Graham Bell. Computers could be quaint little nostalgic memories like hieroglyphics and transistor radios.

We didn't get rich. After the pull tabs it was rubber bands. Made up into balls. She had heard rubber could be sold for top dollar if you had enough of it. We had one ball that was as tall as a man and estimated to weigh over five hundred pounds. I was worried about the floor joists. The local paper came out and took a picture of it: WICHITA WOMAN FINDS SATISFACTION IN RUBBER BAND BALL. After that, we started getting cards and letters from people we didn't even know.

Then it was paper clips, chained together. Looked like a biker convention.

VHS tapes were next. She was convinced that one day they would be highly collectible (she always gave a little emphasis to the word *highly*) and worth real money.

Then she started collecting junk mail. Swear to God.

Junk mail. What she said was that one day, all these sales circulars and pre-approved zero percent interest rate credit card offers and missing children notices and AOL CDs and Publishers Clearinghouse Sweepstakes packets—that one day they would be historical artifacts and she was going to open a museum and charge people to see them.

"Junk mail? That's crazy."

"No, it's not. Think about it."

"I don't need to think about it."

"No. Think about it. Really think about it for a minute. I'm serious. Junk mail. What do people do with junk mail?"

"They throw it the fuck away," is what I said and she kind of blinked at me and that crease that I would become so familiar with made its first appearance.

"Yes," she said, "They throw it the fuck away." Putting a kind of deadpan non-emphasis on the ugly word. "Just pretend like you still love me," she said. "Pretend like you care about what I have to say. Pretend like you still think I'm an intelligent woman whose ideas are worth hearing."

"I'm sorry."

"Well."

"Really. I'm sorry. But they throw it away. That's what people do with their junk mail."

The crease softened. Turned into a little mischievous half-smile. Like I'd fallen into the verbal trap she had set. She said, "Yes, they do. They throw it away. Everybody throws it away. *Everybody.*"

"But not you."

"No. Not me. I'm not stupid, you know. This is for real. There's even a name for it."

Yeah, *crazy*, is what I thought but did not say. It's called being crazy. It's called being a pack rat. It's called living in filth. It's called living your life surrounded by things that normal people throw away. I could hear the cats somewhere off deep in the house, mewling. Sounded like babies crying. I hate cats.

"It's called ephemera. Ephemeron—that's the singular—is paper that was meant to be thrown away. Like cocktail napkins and awards programs and church bulletins and ticket stubs. Collectors pay a lot of money for ephemera. Do you know why?"

"I don't have the first idea."

"They pay a lot of money for ephemera because ephemeron is rare. Do you know why it's so rare?"

Of course, by now, I knew where this was headed, but I just said no, so she could have the satisfaction of making her point. That's what a successful marriage is really all about. Concessions. Making little concessions.

"Ephemeron is rare because it was *made to be thrown away*. It's all been put in the trash. Only just a little bit still exists."

She was stabbing her finger at the air when she said this. Stabbing toward me.

"Like what if you had a playbill from Ford's Theater," she said. "Or even just a ticket stub to see that play that Abraham Lincoln was watching the night he got shot? There were a lot of people there to see that play, but every last one of them probably threw away their ticket stub. 'Cause that's what you do with ticket stubs. If we had one of those stubs, just imagine what it would be worth."

I doubt it would be worth enough to cover your psychiatric bills, is what I thought but did not say.

There were lots of little scenes like that. Tense. Uncomfortable. It got to where I stopped speaking up for fear of seeing that crease.

I started to notice how hard it was just to find a place to sit down and watch TV. There was stuff—highly collectible valuables—stored on every flat surface. We ate our meals standing up because the dining room table was piled high with Beanie Babies and Happy Meal toys and used coloring books (*what if one of those little children grows up to be the next Picasso?*). The chairs were full of ephemera too. Ephemeron. Whatever. Empty cereal boxes and Waylon Jennings 8-track tapes and blow cards from out of magazines and paperback books stripped of their covers and just about any damn thing you could think of.

And I realized that when we walked from one room to another in our house, we were walking along trails. Paths that cut through the trash and clutter. I wasn't able to see it accumulating, just like you can't see snow accumulating. You can only see it after the fact. She piled it and piled it and piled it. Piece by piece. Flake by flake. Molecule by molecule. Carbon, pressure, and time. Grease-stained pizza boxes with fascinating graphics and empty Scotch Tape containers and vintage cat toys and throw pillows and a broken air hockey table and busted speakers and board games that were missing pieces and cracked Christmas ornaments and empty milk jugs. Trash. It was all trash.

As I mentioned, it was a slow process. Gradual. And before long, our home not only had paths and trails that cut through the junk, but the garbage was piled so high we would get from Point A to Point B by crawling through a trash tunnel. A burrow.

There was a period when one of the cats went missing. Couldn't find it anywhere. We could hear it mewling sometimes, like a baby crying. (That's twice I've compared the sound a cat makes to a baby's cries. Our baby died. I should have told you that. It's not something I talk about. We were still newly married. We were both different people then. After it happened, I stayed on the road a lot, and she stayed home. She was home grieving our dead daughter, and I was on the road, searching in the sun for another overload. That changed us. I should have told you that.) I figured the cat was caught somewhere. Probably a pile of trash fell over on it and trapped it or broke its leg or something. After three days the mewling stopped. Then about three days after that, the smell started up. Real subtle at first. I won't describe it. It became intense. So strong that I couldn't sleep at night. But eventually it settled down. Backed off. It was still there, but no longer overpowering. And finally it either stopped smelling or we just got used to living with it. I don't know. That was a pretty good cat, too. Liked to rub up against you and purr and be stroked. Usually, I can't stand cats, but that one was special. I miss her.

Time. And pressure. I blame myself most of all. I should have been stronger. Home more. Because here we are today and she wants to add another cookie sheet to our collection of pots and pans, and I don't have the strength to say no. And even if I did, what would it help at this point? She'll never stop grieving. I understand that. Time is a motherfucker.

She asks me if I will go to her bathroom and get her contact solution so she can clean her lenses. I haven't been to her bathroom in a long time. I just use the guest toilet. But she has been gaining weight and it's hard sometimes for her to squeeze and climb and burrow to get in there. I'm pretty sure that sometimes she pees in a plastic Slurpee cup and pours it down the kitchen sink.

I can hear her singing in the kitchen. It's a happy song, but she sings it in a sad voice. Pretty. There was a time when this house was full with the sound of her singing. So I set off for her bathroom. I was a little worried about it. This place was getting dangerous. I didn't want to end up like that cat. Like our daughter.

It took a while. A lot of crawling, squeezing. Eventually, I emerged into her bathroom. We used to share it. It was the master bath, right off our bedroom. I didn't even see our bedroom getting here. I reckon it's still there.

It had a garden tub and separate freestanding shower.

There was a big walk-in closet off to the side. Secluded toilet area. A long vanity with two sinks. The cat's litter box was under the vanity. Looked like it had been quite some time since it had been emptied. Like since the Carter administration. With one cat gone it didn't fill up as fast, but damn, you still had to change it once in a while. It looked like there were clumps of urine-coagulated litter spread across the countertop, too. Little sand-encrusted doo-doo logs. Bits of tin foil and kite string and cat turds and fast food containers and bags and cups and half-eaten hamburgers and chicken bones and there were even some bones up on the wall, hung there somehow. But not chicken bones. Cat bones. Guess she found Cuddles after all. And there was the—I guess you'd call it the pelt—hung up there too. And there was something red and white and fluffy strung up on wire and yarn across the mirror. Almost like homemade Christmas ornaments with snow and red icing. And pretty quick I realized those were tampons. Used tampons and sanitary napkins strung up there with cat bones and a pelt and all I could think was, I am so afraid of dying.

Somewhere, real far away, I could hear singing. Like a child singing. A little tinkling musical voice. But sad.

And the wire and yarn and string were twisted up, fibrous, and coming off the mirror into her walk-in closet. It was deep in there. Parts unknown. I could see the stars. My God, the stars. I followed the line, and I saw she had woven some of those used Kotex into it, too. Blood. I thought about the little girl who cut her finger and lost her arm, and I thought about diamonds raining down from the sky. Pressure. And time. It was blood and string and wire. And cat guts. Glistening with Vaseline or something. All of it woven into a cord. A line. A line leading into the stars. It was humming. I could feel it in my teeth. The whine of it.

And I could hear her singing in the wire.

I could hear her through the whine.

I am the Wichita lineman.

And I'm still on the line.

HIGHWAYMAN
(A PLACE TO REST YOUR SPIRIT)

It was raining today, but Freddie stuck to his usual lunch routine. He left the office at 12:15 and hit the Wendy's drive-thru. He ordered two junior bacon cheeseburgers and a large Dr. Pepper—no ice. As always.

He parked his Honda Civic at the outskirts of a Home Depot parking lot. Where they had constructed full-scale samples of the storage sheds they had for sale. Freddie found those sheds to be quite relaxing, and so every day, rain or shine, he parked here, facing them while he ate his lunch and listened to music. Relaxing. There was just something about those sheds.

On the radio, The Highwaymen—Johnny Cash, Waylon Jennings, Willie Nelson, and Kris Kristofferson—were singing a song about reincarnation, and Freddie listened to them on low while he unwrapped his first burger. Willie Nelson sang the opening verse, about robbing people along the highway, back in the 1600s or something, and how they hung him for it, but he was still alive.

Freddie sucked some Dr. Pepper up through the straw and watched the tapering rain. He tried not to think about the knapsack in the backseat. He chose to focus on pleasant thoughts. The thing about those sheds was that they looked like little houses. With cottage windows and shingled roofs. Like little miniature houses, not garden sheds.

Kris Kristofferson was recalling how he had sailed a schooner in another life and got killed climbing the mast in a storm. But he was still alive.

The rain was kind of misting now, trickling down the windshield.

The junior bacon cheeseburgers were good today. Sometimes the bacon was stale. You could get one of the smaller sheds for less than a thousand dollars. Freddie imagined setting one down in the woods somewhere and maybe somehow running a power line out to it. They were just like little houses. And you could live out there in the woods and have radio for music, and even a TV. You would have to go outside to use the bathroom, but that was fine. It added to the appeal.

Waylon Jennings sang about being a construction worker on the Boulder Dam, and falling off it and being buried in a tomb of wet cement. But he was still alive.

One time, Freddie got out of his car and walked into one of those sheds. It was a deluxe four-thousand-dollar model that had stairs inside leading up to a loft with a little balustrade. He stood up there, looking out the window at his car in the parking lot, and imagined himself living in the shed, out in the middle of nowhere, snow swirling in the bitter cold outside, but him warm inside. Then he felt nervous and had a bowel movement in the corner of the loft. It was probably still up there.

Johnny Cash finished the song up. He sang about being out in the universe, out amongst the stars. A place to rest your spirit. And Freddie thought: *The stars. My God, the stars.* Johnny sang about being reincarnated all over again as a highwayman. Or just coming back as a raindrop. But he would still be alive.

Freddie balled up the burger wrappers and finished off the Dr. Pepper. It felt good to be full.

He got out of the car and carried the knapsack through the drizzle to his favorite shed. He climbed upstairs. The turd was still up there. Mummified, but recognizable for what it was. He took the rope out of the pack. It really did feel good to be full. Freddie wondered what the medical examiner would make of that when they inspected the contents of his stomach.

Once he had the free end of the rope secured to a rafter, he put the noose around his neck and scooted off the loft railing. Freddie was lucky. The freefall was just barely enough to snap his neck. His body ticked in front of the cottage window that was oh-so warm and homey.

In the few fleeting seconds that were left to him in this life, Freddie's protruding eyes looked out the window and watched the mist collect on the windshield of his car. Where it beaded up into single raindrops and rolled down the glass.

THE STARRY NIGHT

ONE

The stars. My God, the stars.

Is what Mr. Landay thought as he looked out the living room window and contemplated his plan. The swirling nighttime sky. The universe expanding. He imagined Vincent van Gogh, in all his self-injurious, bugfuck crazy glory, had gazed upon much the same sight outside his asylum window those many years ago.

Mr. Landay had given his plan a great deal of thought. He was a careful man. And a patient man. He learned patience from the stars. The stars abide.

Mr. Landay had no intention of ever getting caught.

For starters, Mr. Landay never perused his interests online. Never. That was the number one no-no as far as Mr. Landay was concerned. He simply did not understand these men who pursued their hobby in chatrooms and message boards, or via instant messages and texts and photo exchanges and the myriad other electronic ways in which children could be had. Tricked, mislead, blackmailed, etc. Why, you couldn't even turn on the news without seeing some weak-chinned schmo with an uneven goatee blinking under the hot lights. Caught. Caught red-handed meeting up with a child he'd enticed online. Why weren't people more careful? Discreet?

If it wasn't that, then it was footage of FBI agents carrying hard drives out of homes to catalog the caches of thousands upon thousands of illegal images their forensic technicians divined from the digital depths of said hard drives. Then the feds sifted through your contacts and next thing you knew they would say you were part of an organization. A child molestation ring. And if one of your fellow hobbyists happened to live in Canada or something, then they would be crowing about you being the lynchpin in an international ring of child pornographers. And when would people learn the simple art of discretion? The stars, the planets. They were discreet. The universe was discreet.

Mr. Landay was a big believer in discretion. Discretion was an art, and Mr. Landay an artist.

The Internet was not safe. It had never been safe. If you used the Internet, you would be caught.

The downside to discretion was that one did not get the opportunity to wallow in one's basest desires. Chances to indulge those proclivities—safe chances— were few and far between.

Over the years, Mr. Landay had experienced some mild successes. Nothing epic, though. He was still waiting for the one experience that would define him. Someone to be Ryan O'Neal to his Ali MacGraw. There had been a neighbor boy whom he'd caught setting fires. Blackmailed him. That had lasted almost three months.

Until the boy's family had moved away. Even though the boy remained emotionally detached (perhaps clinically so), Mr. Landay missed him. He had been deeply troubled, and Mr. Landay hoped he would find peace in this world.

There were the twins. Alicia and Alice. His sister's girls. But he'd never felt right about that. It had been wrong. And he was certain they'd been too young to remember. If they did remember, they certainly gave no indication when he saw them over the holidays. Although Alice was apparently a lesbian now. Transgendered. Something like that. And Alicia was filling her skin with tattoos. Just filling herself up, inking herself like she thought human beings were blank coloring books in need of a crayon.

Unlike some, Mr. Landay did not differentiate between boys and girls. All that mattered was their essence. Their goodness. Their scent. The smell of children. He inhaled it. Savored it. He was driven. Compelled. Even though he knew he would spend eternity in hell (deservedly so), it was worth it.

He could not stop. But he could be careful. Safe.

Mr. Landay had worked at the hospital in a janitorial capacity for all of his adult life. Environmental Services. It was a good job with decent pay, and he had taken on more and more responsibilities over the years, so that he now supervised the safe disposal of biohazard and infectious waste materials—he ran the incinerator.

He oversaw the destruction by fire of bloody gauze, pus-filled dressings, urine-soaked pads, biopsied tissue samples, excised tumors, aborted fetuses, amputated fingers toes hands breasts limbs etc. He went from floor to floor gathering red bags and sharps boxes onto his special cart. During busy times, when the combustion chamber never even got to cool down between loads, the different departments brought the red bags down to him. Delivered them to him. And all he had to do was keep the temperature up to state regs and keep an eye on the exhaust readouts and keep the numbers within BACT and MACT air standards.

The blue Moss Incinerator had been upgraded and computerized some few years back, so that now much of those environmental and regulatory standards were kept within limits by the computer. Fluid levels, air injection, HHV's, airborne particulate. All of it was automated. But Mr. Landay had had the higher ups thinking that he alone was qualified to keep the fire breathing dragon in line. Job security. He called himself a specialist in the field of biomedical waste management, but in reality he was nothing more than a bumpkin with a pitch fork and burning barrel.

It had crossed his mind that if he ever got into a situation in which things got out of control—for whatever reason—then he would have an out. He would have a way to destroy the evidence. It was funny. Even though Mr. Landay understood that he was a diseased human being, he was still essentially human, and most people's initial reactions were just like his when viewing the incinerator for the first time. They had the same thought that he'd had when he'd first seen it. Invariably they asked Mr. Landay if he thought the big blue steel Moss Incinerator could be used to destroy the evidence of a murder. And Mr. Landay always told them what old Mr. Kennestone had told him in his shaky old-man voice when he trained Mr. Landay on the pre-upgraded machine many years ago: It would cook you. Cook you down to bones.

Mr. Landay did not think it would ever come to that. Hoped not. He was not that kind of man.

Although there had been opportunities over the years, chances for quick and unseemly grope sessions, or even long cons to build parasitic relationships with ill or injured children and their parents (single mothers were prime opportunities, single mothers of sick children were begging for exploitation), Mr. Landay had not sought to indulge his peculiar proclivities via his position at the hospital. Don't shit where you eat. Don't get high on your own supply. Etcetera and so forth.

Play it safe. That was his motto. His parents were still alive. And the thought of his mother or father becoming aware that their son was a monster, well, that was just too much. Play it safe. And that's what he had done. Until just recently.

He had seen an opportunity. A glorious opportunity.

Since there were times when orderlies and aides and the like in various departments throughout the hospital were tasked with gathering the red bag biohazard materials from their respective departments and delivering the infectious waste items to Mr. Landay for incineration, he was brought into contact with a wide range of low-level employees.

There was one young woman in particular, a little retarded girl who worked in the Children's Cancer and Blood Disorder Clinic. A sweet thing. Retarded. A little short plump roly-poly of a thing. Amy. Her mind was as simple and clear as the sky over a Nebraska cornfield. Mr. L was drawn to her. To her innocence. To her child-like nature.

A friendship blossomed between them. She often came downstairs and ate lunch with Mr. L, scribbling in her diary while the two of them ate near the cardboard baler, their table a compressed cube of empty boxes. She just scribbled away in her hot pink Hello Kitty Dream Diary. That's what she did. "I a writer," is what she told him. Cute.

And he could tell she was sort of dressing up for him. Bright pink eyeshadow with sparkles in it. Pink sparkly polish on her nails. Stardust. That's what she called it. Pink stardust. Poor thing. Looked garish. Clownlike. Stardust indeed. Billion year old carbon.

And it would have been a simple thing to capitalize on that friendship. To gain and then betray her trust. To convince her to do things for him in the name of their friendship. She would do anything to avoid offending him. To avoid hurting her friend's feelings. Oh, the things he could make her do by manipulating her emotions. It would have been so easy. But, in the end, although she was innocent and like a child in so many ways, she simply was not a child. Physically, she was an adult woman. She did not smell like a child. She did not have a child's body. A child's mind, yes, but Mr. Landay required the whole package. He was not one to settle.

And so Mr. Landay was unable to perceive how his position at the hospital could help in that particular area of his life. Until last month. Something had happened when staffing was tight, and Mr. Landay was required to go up into the hospital and retrieve the red bag materials from the various floors.

He had been pushing his stainless steel cart through the Children's Cancer Clinic, gathering red bags like a migrant field worker, plucking up a bumper crop of sharps boxes. He stopped and chatted with Amy. And he lingered. He lingered because the entire floor smelled of children. It was an olfactory overload. He could happily live his life out in such an environment.

And as he lingered and chatted and savored, Mr. Landay noticed something. Something caught his eye. He'd seen this thing many times before, but the ramifications of it had never struck fully home. Until now.

Mr. Landay noticed that inside this fortress of a hospital with its privacy and security measures firmly in place, inside a children's ward in which a single adult male would be eyed with suspicion, would be asked countless times, *may I help you, sir?* Within all of this, there was a certain group of individuals who had free rein. There was a class of people on this floor who could come and go as they pleased, unchallenged. A type of person who had complete access to every child in the clinic—no ID or employee badge required. They were allowed to approach children and interact with them and build relationships and gain their trust. To forge alliances with children who were sick and completely dependent up adult intervention and guidance.

There was a way that Mr. Landay could walk onto this floor in complete and utter anonymity and never be questioned as to the nature of his presence here. And if by chance he ever was challenged, asked to provide ID, he could say that he left it in his street clothes, go out to retrieve it, and never come back.

It took him a month of carefully examining his plan from every possible angle before he actually accepted that it was as foolproof as he believed it to be. This was the opportunity of a lifetime, the stars had truly aligned, and Mr. Landay was damned if he was going to let it pass him by.

Once he was sure, he went out and purchased the necessary supplies. And he placed "emergency kits" in various hidey holes throughout the hospital. Just in case. Always have a plan B.

And if anyone ever did become suspicious, if there ever was any danger of detection, why he had an eye on the inside, didn't he? He had Amy. She wouldn't let him down.

TWO

I a writer. Down sindome. I a writer. I a retarded. I work here. I Amy. I work here hospital little kids. I a retarded. I used work to the workshop with other retardeds. Put together piece metal make things. Miss Brooks-Lane she get me job hospital. I love the little kids. I love babies. I love Miss Brooks-Lane. Thank you Miss Brooks-Lane.

I love the babies the little children. They sick. My god they sick. The little children. They have the cancer. I a retarded. The little children they love me. They have the cancer. In they blood. In they brain. In they bones. Lukeemia. The little kids be bald no hair. I work here. I help them. They say I help them. They love me. I get paid. Paycheck. Twice week month. Mr. Crandell my supervisor. He nice. Funny. Make Amy laugh. He bald too no hair like children. But no cancer. He say his hair fall out. He say his hair saw his face got scared run away. He funny. I love Mr. Crandell too. He married man name Kip. Funny.

I get paid. Paycheck. No more workshop. I get paid. Sometime I hold the hand little children when they put the needle. Little children no like needle. Amy no like needle. Amy be brave little children. It hurt. It hurt bad. The little children cry. The Mommy Daddy cry too. They all cry. I hold they hand too. They feel better. I get paycheck. Paid. Twice week month. I have bank account. Checkcard. Visa.

Sometime no stop baby mommy daddy cry. I no stop. I take picture my phone. Everybody smile picture. That my secret. Everybody smile picture. Get it? Mr. Crandell say delete HIPAA. Privacy. No picture break rule privacy HIPAA. I say okay delete. But it work. Stop little children crying mommy daddy too. Smile.

Mr. Crandell funny. Ha ha. Jokes. I love him. Bald.

The cancer everywhere. Little children. My god they sick. I sad. Cry at night alone sometime I think about it. No cry at work. I strong. Get paid.

The clown come to the cancer clinic. Lots of clown. Boy clown. Girl clown. Sometime I no tell boy or girl clown. Just clown. I no like the clown. Why clown? Sometime little children cry see clown. Scared clown. Why clown for cancer? No understand.

One clown come in. Bad clown. Man clown. No see his face. You no see his face. He be anybody. Nobody ask see his badge. Nobody ask see his picture card who he is. Nobody ask see band on wrist. No band. He could be anybody. Why nobody ask who that clown? I ask. Who that clown? Who that clown? I no like that clown.

The mommy and daddy and little baby go in tranfoosion room. Where they stick the needle good medicine that kill the cancer make hair fall out. Hurt make baby sick but kill the cancer. The mommy daddy they worried about they little baby no see they little child daughter go off. She go walk around. No want to see needle. They have video game all over place. Ms. Pacman. Galaga. Free. No quarter. It free. And anybody can play for free and sometime I play Ms. Pac-man for free and Mr. Crandell say we no pay Amy to play video game. He say get back to work. But it okay for Amy to play video game with the little children. That why I here. Make friend. Make feel good. Make no think about cancer.

Sometime too I empty trash and take BIOHAZARD downstair Mr. Landay burn it up. Safe. He my friend too. He no funny but talk Amy make feel good. Important. He no treat retarded. And too I put toilet paper bathroom. Sometime rubber glove give nurse pee-pee cup left in bathroom. Rubber glove. Latex. But I hold people hand picture take make feel better. Smile. That my job. I get paid. Help people. Check. My name.

The little girl daughter she walk around. The mommy daddy worry about baby boy needle in his arm bag of likwid medicine take long time put all that medicine in little arm. Sad. I sad for them.

Daughter she play Ms. Pac-man like me. I play with her little bit. That okay. I be friend to her. I make people feel good welcome Mr. Crandell say okay.

Bad clown he watch us.

I have the down sindome. I say that already. Eyes slant look in mirror. Chinese. I a retarded. I know.

Mr. Crandell say go downstair get more special wipe they use to clean. BIOHAZARD. Mr. Crandell say get more. I get more.

Bad clown watch me get on elevator. He watch the daughter girl. Her mommy daddy no watch her. They no watch her. I no watch her. Elevator. She alone.

I come back. Special wipes. ANTIMICROBIAL. The clown he gone. The daughter girl she gone. Then Amy see daughter girl. She cry. She sad tears. The mommy daddy they think tears baby cancer. No baby cancer. No. Daughter girl cry clown. Daughter girl cry clown.

Bad clown gone.

Bad clown back. Another day. Bad clown back. He bad.

Nobody see clown. Notice. They think normal. I no think normal. I think bad. Amy notice. Amy see.

Boy with cancer. Brain. Bald head stitches. Boy head stitches like baseball. Clown friend boy. Galaga. No boy. Clown no friend.

I tell Mr. Crandell bad clown. I say Mr. Crandell that clown bad no good. Mr. Crandell think I scared clowns. I no scared clowns. He bad clown. I tell. I tell him. Mr. Crandell no understand retarded words. Amy not talk good. Some people scared clowns he say. It okay he say.

It not okay.

I spy clown. Amy watch. Follow.

He in bathroom with boy. Little metal door in bathroom wall. I know. Sometime Amy get pee pee cup for nurse. Rubber glove. Universe precaution. Use metal door. They leave pee pee cup in wall.

I go other side of metal door. Nurse area. I open little metal door. No pee pee cup. I no supposed open both door see inside bathroom. Wrong. Privacy. HIPAA.

I open both door. See inside. No see anything. I put my phone camera through. Stick arm through. All the way. Amy take picture.

I do wrong. Amy do bad wrong. Privacy. HIPAA. They told me privacy. Respect. I look at picture. Bad picture. Bad wrong. Nasty.

What do? What do? I break rule. No want get fire. Miss Brooks-Lane disappoint in me. She get me job. No want get fire. Amy love my job. Paycheck. Help people. I a writer.

Clown see me look at picture. I look at him. He look at me. He know. I know.

He try talk me. Say see pretty picture. He say he help little children feel good. Like me. He no like me. He say what your name. Amy. He say you pretty Amy. You want go get candy. He talk like I a retarded.

I scared. I think Mr. Landay.

THREE

This was very, very, very bad. Likely the worse ever. Mr. Landay had been caught. Red handed. Caught by his friend, Amy. In flagrante delicto. Photographic evidence. In blazing offence. The retarded girl need only push the wrong button and that photograph would be bouncing around in outer space, circling the globe ten times over before Mr. Landay could draw even a single breath. Very bad indeed. Mr. Landay had never been in such a predicament.

Of course he recognized Amy's sparkly nail polish (*stardust*) as soon as the hand holding the phone had emerged cobralike through the sample pass-through door. The dual-access biological safety cabinet. The chart room, he knew, was on the other side. The pink iPhone with its sparkly skin. There was even time to see the phone display the captured image on its four-inch widescreen high resolution retina display. It was strikingly clear. A little off center. A bit tilted. But the focus was spot on, the clarity alarming. It was bad, very bad indeed.

He left the boy behind. No need to smooth the edges. No need to speak to him one last time of that special bond they shared. The need for secrecy. Of how his parents were already under unbearable strain worrying about the boy's cancer, etcetera, etcetera, so forth and so on. No, no need for any of that refinery. The jig was up. What he needed was to get the hell out of here before sweet precious Amy started showing that photograph to anyone who was willing to indulge the demands of a little retarded woman.

The immediate task at hand was to get off this floor before he was stopped and questioned. He would never be back here again. This was a dead socket to him now. A black hole. The immediate task at hand was damage control. First get off the floor. And it might be that was all he needed. For, really, what did Amy have? She had a photograph of a boy and a clown. Engaged in inappropriate behavior. A clown and a boy. It had nothing to do with Mr. L. He still had his anonymity. He was pretty sure. It all depended on Amy.

He was an unidentified man in oversize floppy shoes, an orange shock wig, red bulbous nose, Liza Minnelli eyebrows, and heavy white greasepaint. Unrecognizable. Untraceable. Unless. Unless Amy had somehow recognized him. As he had recognized her sparkly fingernails. Unless there was a tell of some kind. But he didn't think there was. He was a careful man.

She was retarded, but she was perceptive in her way.

He had to know. Before he got off this floor, he had to know if she recognized him. And it wouldn't be a bad idea to destroy that phone.

Mr. Landay walked past nurses and aides and phlebotomists and oncologists and hematologists and he took the time to toot his little plastic horn at some of the children. And even in his current state, he was aware of the fragrance they were giving off. Then he saw her. Ahead, in the elevator vestibule. Amy. Looking at that damn phone. She looked up at him. He looked at her. There was fear in her puffy, slanted eyes. Anger too, it looked like. And maybe recognition. Was that recognition? Did she recognize him? He had to know.

Mr. Landay knelt down beside Amy and asked if he could see the pretty picture. She shook her head in defiance. And Mr. Landay had a sense that this girl could be capable of violence. Amy. Violence. Not possible, he once would have thought.

"What's your name, pretty girl?" Mr. Landay asked. Soothing.

"Amy." It was a bark. A bark from a dog warning off a bigger predator.

"There's a candy machine downstairs. Can I buy you a candy bar? I was only trying to help the sick boy. Like you do."

The control panel dinged and Mr. Landay and Amy both looked up to see the elevator doors whoosh open. Then, without realizing what had happened, Mr. Landay was flat on his back, sprawled across the floor. Amy had pushed him. Hard. She had, as they used to say back in school, knocked him on his ass.

He tilted his head to watch her walk into the elevator. Her Hello Kitty Dream Diary and pink-skinned iPhone clutched to her bosom. And those mongoloid eyes of hers were heavy lidded with defiance.

The doors closed and Mr. Landay picked himself up. There were people around, but no one seemed overly concerned with a fallen clown. He watched the lighted display cycle through the floor numbers as the elevator descended. Cycling lower and lower. But it did not stop at the first floor where Hospital administration was housed and Amy could have found any number of interested parties with whom to share her multi-media presentation. Nor did it stop at M where security officers and other Personnel milled about and the cafeteria drew all manner of people. And on past L it went, where once again the good people of the world would be anxious to hear her tale. The elevator ultimately stopped at the very last destination available. LL.

Lower Level. Landay Land.

And it finally dawned on him. As though God had intervened on Mr. Landay's behalf. God loved all his children equally. Mr. L understood that now. A smile perched on his blood-red lips. Not only did she not recognize him in the clown makeup, but Amy was actually going to the Lower Level to seek comfort and solace from her good friend, Mr. Landay.

He punched the wall button with his white-gloved finger to call the elevator up. He had to hurry. He wasn't even sure where the stairs were. He wasn't a young man anymore, in any case. A little Mexican girl and her family wandered up and waited for the elevator with him. Probably going downstairs for a bite to eat. The little girl was pushing a rolling IV stand. Her chemotherapy. The elevator arrived, but he didn't want them witnessing his destination. As he pushed the girl out of his way, the IV tubing popped free from the venous catheter in her arm, spraying little droplets of poison. She started crying.

Mr. L's eyes twinkled with genuine delight under his arc de triumph eyebrows as the elevator descended. He got off on seven, where he had stashed a bag of necessities in the acoustic tiled ceiling of a seldom-used bathroom just outside Bariatrics.

He was already feeling better. The situation could be contained. He thought of the swirling stars, the universe expanding, and he knew that in a very real sense the outcome had already been decided. Poor Amy. This had already happened and would happen again. Faulkner was right. The past isn't dead. It's not even past. Van Gogh knew it too. And so did Mr. Landay.

Poor Amy. Maybe she knew it too.

FOUR

I think Mr. Landay. He help Amy.

It cold down here. Amy scared. Nervous.

Mr. Landay help me. He my friend. Mr. Landay listen Amy. Where Mr. Landay? He no here. I sit. I write. I look picture on phone. Bad picture. I put it Facebook? No. Nasty. I wait Mr. Landay. He help Amy.

I get lonely. Scared. Where Mr. Landay? Me leave. Show Mr. Crandell. Mr. Crandell mad about HIPAA. Patient privacy. No picture. I tell. I better not show Mr. Crandell nasty. I write. I wait. Long time. Need help.

Somebody come. I hear. I see. Mr. Landay. Everything be ok. Amy feel better.

"Amy! How you doing, sunshine?"

Mr. Landay call me sunshine. I like. "Mr. Landay, I got trouble. Big trouble."

Mr. Landay understand retarded words. Some people no understand Amy.

"Big trouble? Oh no! Maybe I can help. I bet I can. You just sit right here at my desk."

Mr. Landay desk piece wood two block. He funny sometime. Sometime no. He burn trash. BIOHAZARD. I give Mr. Landay phone. He look see.

"Bad clown touch boy."

"Bad clown, indeed. Although I don't think he's actually touching him. No, it looks to me more like he just wants to be close. Yes, I think that's all it is. He just wants—now, Amy, did you get permission to take this photograph?"

"No sir, no permission. Bad clown hurt boy."

"No, no, I really don't think he's hurting the boy. Are you sure the clown wasn't just a doctor dressed up like that?"

"Doctor?"

"Yes, they do that sometimes. Dress up like clowns. I thought you knew. Did you show this to anyone?"

Mr. Landay hand me back phone. "No. I no show."

"Not even Mr. Crandell?"

"No. He get mad. HIPAA."

"There's something wrong with his hip? He hurt himself? I hope he and that, uhm, Kip fellow, didn't overdo it."

"No. Not hip. Hip-ah. Private. HIPAA."

"Oh, yes, yes, yes. Health Information Privacy something something. I'd forgotten about that. I'm afraid this photograph is a clear violation of HIPAA policy. A clear violation. I hate to say this, Amy, but you could lose your job."

"Love job. Paycheck. Help people. Love job."

"I know dear, but if anybody ever found out you took this photograph, it would mean automatic termination. You just can't take pictures of people using the bathroom."

"Termnation?"

"Dismissal—you'd be fired. No job."

Amy grab Mr. Landay. Hold him. I cry. I cry. Can't help. I cry. Say, "Please no tell, Mr. Landay. Please no tell. I do anything. No tell. Amy do anything."

Mr. Landay push Amy back. Look in Amy eye. He say Amy I no tell. He say Amy I no tell but we break phone camera be sure.

"You see the wisdom, don't you? If we destroy the phone, no one will ever know."

Delete, I say. Delete. Easy. Show how.

"No, I'm afraid that's just not good enough. These things hold onto information. You just can't trust them. Believe me, I know, Amy."

Mr. Landay walk across room. He push button on big metal fire maker. Loud buzz. It whoosh. Rumble. Fire.

"I'm afraid we have to burn it, Amy. It's the only way to be sure."

"No want to."

"You want to keep your job?"

"Yes. Job keep."

"You want Mr. Crandell to call the HIPAA authorities?"

"No."

"Because if he does, and they confiscate your phone and find that photograph, you could end up behind bars."

"Bars? Amy?"

"What I'm saying is Amy go jail."

Burn phone I say and give phone. No want phone. Want everything be okay again. Be over. Bad day. Bad clown. Over.

Mr. Landay throw phone in fire. Metal door bang shut it scare Amy.

"That's it, Amy. It's all over. Like it never happened. Everything normal. Never speak of this again. If you pretend that it never happened, then it never did. Okay?"

Okay okay okay I say okay grab hold Mr. Landay love him happy he help Amy no trouble gone. Give big hug. I squeeze. He no like touch. It okay. I give big hug. I see white paint behind Mr. Landay ear. I touch. I show white finger Mr. Landay. Oh my he say. He say oh my.

I say white like clown. Bad clown. Mr. Landay?

Oh Amy Mr. Landay say. He sad. I see he sad. I no

wish you do that he say. I say sorry white paint like clown face.

Then I no breath. Amy no breath. Mr. Landay he choke Amy. Hands hurt. No breath. Hurt. Why? I no understand. Amy a retarded. Why? He squeeze. Amy no breath. Face hot. Tired. Sleepy. No breath. I look. I see Mr. Landay eyes. They dark. Amy sleepy. Eyes like night. So dark. I get lost. Mr. Landay eyes. Dark. Swallow Amy up. Amy lost in the dark. See specks light. Dots light in the dark. The stars. Amy see the stars. They swurl turn. Stars. My God.

FIVE

Mr. Landay was crying. It was just so unutterably sad. Poor Amy. Poor dead thing. He never thought any of it would ever come to this. Yet on some level, he must have, because he had planned for it, hadn't he? He planned for everything. Plan B. Plan C. Plan D. So forth and so on. But even though he'd planned for it, given it thought, he'd never considered himself capable. He in fact had no idea if he was capable of that kind of violence until right this minute. But he was. He was. Poor Amy. A sweet soul.

Mr. Landay cracked the torpedo-hatch door on the big blue Moss. It was still hot inside. He set about cleaning off some carbon deposits clinging to the walls of the combustion chamber. He wanted Amy to have a clean burn. Carbon. That's all we are. Stardust.

He set the solution level to the hottest burn possible.

Everything looked good. The Old Blue Lady, that's what he called her. She could handle a lot. But she couldn't handle a whole adult body just tossed in there. No. He would have to feed it smaller pieces. Break the load down and send it in inside the stainless steel cart. He put on his surgical mask and gown as was correct protocol when dealing with bio-medical waste. In the toolbox he found a hacksaw and a hammer that would be good for the bones. That should do it. Whatever was left after incineration he could run through the sharps shredder.

It was just that his parents were still alive. Mr. Landay simply couldn't risk getting caught. Bringing shame to them. He was sorry for Amy. So sorry. But it wasn't like killing a regular human being. Amy was Amy. Maybe they would meet again. Out there in the universe. Their carbon mingling.

He went to check the solution levels and air feed to the secondary chamber one last time before he set about the task of reducing Amy.

SIX

I wake up. Floor cold. Dirty. I miss the stars. Stars wake me up. Stars make me sleep. Swurling. I alive. I Amy. Throat hurt. Bad. Mr. Landay stand over fire door. Buzzing. Whoosh. Loud. He bad. Kill Amy. Choke hurt. No breathe. Dark eyes. See stars. Touch boy. Touch girl. Bad clown. Kill Amy. Burn me up. I know. He burn Amy. Gone.

I get up. Amy get up. Amy not scared. Amy mad.

Mad. I mad. Little children. Cancer. Throat hurt. Swallow. Hurt. See Mr. Landay. Mr. Landay stand front fire. Senterator. I run. Push. I push. Push hard. Mr. Landay look at Amy. He surprise. Eyes big. Dark. No stars. Him fingers grab hold edge door. Hold on. I push again. Harder. Mr. Landay hold on. He scared. He say Amy. No Amy. Amy stop. Please Amy stop. I hurt. He say I hurt. Mr. Landay hurt. Please Amy. Sweet girl. He call Amy sweet girl. I let go help Mr. Landay. He my friend. He kick Amy. Trick. Kick Amy private part no man touch tell Mama. It hurt. Hurt bad. Amy private part no man touch tell Mama hurt bad. Mr. Landay smile. He say word Amy no understand. Ugly word. He come at Amy. Hit kick punch swing. Mean. Crazy.

I see hammer floor. Amy pick up hammer. Amy swing. Hit. Right between the eyes. Hit hard. Blood. Bone break. Mr. Landay fall backward. He fall. Fall into metal door. Senterator. Fire. Mr. Landay fire scream. Shut door. Amy shut door. But Mr. Landay loud. Scream. Clown scream. Burn him up. HIPAA okay. I tell Mr. Crandell. He funny.

Amy sad. Amy happy. Amy tired. What happen? Amy sit down. Tired. Throat hurt. Finger hurt. Finger broke. Fingernail broke. Broke off. Stardust. Burn up.

I Amy. I a retarded. Down Sindome. I Amy. I a writer.

SEVEN

A small, hooded, stainless steel pipe jutted from the south wall of the hospital like a miniature smokestack. It emitted the exhaust of the Moss Incinerator. And on that day, fine airborne particulate (2.5 µm diameter), of Mr. Landay was released into the atmosphere.

Mr. Landay was free. He was elemental. Molecular. Reduced.

And those elements were swept into the updraft created by the main tower of the hospital and the neighboring Women's Health Care Center. Up, up, and away. Caught in a warm air front that was bringing thunderstorms to the area. Mr. L was up there for quite some time. Several months. He traveled the globe. Various weather patterns all played a part as he was buffeted about, and it seemed those particulates of Mr. Landay were headed for the stratosphere, where he would become part of the ozone layer and contribute to planetary climate change. But fate interceded, and water vapor condensed on the particulate. Mr. L fell to earth microscopically embedded in a snowflake, where he remained frozen for hundreds of thousands of years, as part of the polar ice cap. When the world's ice fields, glaciers, and ice sheets melted, he remained in the earth's water cycle, until absorbed by a fish, thus riding along the food chain, the end result of which was death, said result ending with Mr. Landay in a decomposing sea creature, embedded in silt on the ocean floor, where he remained for eons. Even as the ocean morphed into a desert and back again, Mr. Landay remained, fossilized, a permanent part of the earth's crust.

Until the day many millions of years later when the earth was struck by a rogue planet, roughly the size of

Venus, barreling through the Milky Way galaxy. The released energy of the impact destroyed both planets. Pulverized them. It was quite impressive.

The chunks of rock, debris, vapor, and dust were not able to regain their binding gravity and coalesce.

All of earth scattered into space.

And thereby did the remaining atoms of Mr. Landay circulate the Virogo Supercluster in a green/blue/orange cosmic dust cloud for well over seven billion years. And if those carbon atoms had a consciousness, they would have thought: *The stars. My God, the stars.* For it was a sight to see.

The nebula was eventually drawn into a solar-system-swallowing black hole in the center of a supergiant elliptical galaxy. The singularity had a mass of 6.6 billion solar masses. Again, quite impressive. A sight to see.

And thus did Mr. Landay enter the gravitational singularity, where spacetime was believed to be infinite. And that my friends, is a long time. But, as has been previously stated, Mr. Landay was a patient man. And he had better be, because his journey had only just begun.

On the other side of the black hole (and, yes, there really is an *other side*—other sides beyond number), many complex and not fully understood processes were at work, but for our purposes here, we can think of what lies at the end of a black hole (as we understand the word *end*, which really isn't entirely applicable here) as a sort of revolving birthing room for galaxies. Let it be known that cosmic dust and gases did gather and collect in sufficient mass that they began to collapse, and gravity pushed the atoms together causing nuclear fusion. A star winked into existence.

Protoplanetery discs formed from the remaining debris and found their orbits around the new sun.

The discs grew bigger, absorbing all material in their paths. Some of that material was carbon atoms that had once been Mr. Landay. The planets grew to maturity. One planet, the largest, was composed of nothing but hydrogen and helium with sixteen moons in orbit around it. Another was a moonless, waterless, sphere of barren rock with an atmosphere of carbon dioxide and sulfur gases with daytime temperatures well above 800 degrees.

It just so happened that the planet that contained Mr. Landay's atoms also held the ingredients that made life possible. Just the right mixture of carbon, hydrogen, nitrogen, oxygen, phosphorus, sulfur and other beneficial components, and was also just the right distance from the sun, so that, some 500 million years later, once it had sufficiently cooled and certain serendipitous circumstances aligned, a carbon-based, single-cell life form emerged.

These single-cell life forms would be quite alone for the next billion-and-a-half years, when multicellular life would evolve. Then plants. Photosynthesis. Finally, animal life.

And it was good.

It all took quite a long time, depending upon one's perspective. All sorts of amazing things happened—and we're skipping over quite a bit—but ultimately, upright, intelligent beings became the dominant life form. And they hurt each other in unspeakable ways. Waged wars. Killed, tortured, and enslaved each other merely for worshiping the wrong god, having the wrong color skin, or simply to indulge their basest desires. As if the random-fate-chaos of the universe weren't already enough of a burden for them to bear—living in a world where famine and disease were everyday occurrences. A world where children got cancer and died.

But these beings also saw and appreciated beauty. Created beauty, as well. They called it art. And one of these beings, an artist, insane as defined by his peers— bugfuck crazy you could say—looked out his window and saw the nighttime sky. Swirling. *Swurling.* The universe expanding. And he saw what no living thing should ever be burdened to see. He saw it all. Swirling. Expanding. Infinite. He alone saw it all.

And he thought: *The stars. My God, the stars.*

YOU ARE NOT HERE

Here is what we know.

We know that at some point between one and three in the morning, Juliet Cook got out of her bed and left her sleeping husband behind. We do not know what woke her, or what prompted her to get out of bed. We do not even know for certain that she had truly been asleep that night. It is possible she only pretended to sleep.

We know that she (or an unknown someone with her—highly unlikely) opened the garage and drove away. She did not close the garage door. And she was still wearing her nightgown.

Juliet's husband, Steven Cook, awoke at three in the morning to find his wife was not in bed, not anywhere in the house, her car gone, and the garage door open. Her cell phone was charging on the kitchen counter. Mr. Cook dressed and took his vehicle to go looking for his wife in the frigid night. He searched for three hours. When he got home, the police were waiting for him. Juliet's car had been found abandoned in the middle of the Walt Whitman Bridge, the driver's door wide open, the engine still running—exhaust swirling.

Her body washed up on the bank of the Delaware River the next day.

This is what we know. What we do not know is why.

Why would a woman with no history of depression or any other mental illness, a woman who was not despondent in any way, a woman who gave no indication whatsoever of suicidal ideations—why would she feel such a sudden and undeniable compulsion to end her own life? A compulsion so urgent that she left her car in the middle of a bridge, idling, with the door open? What compelled her?

This question haunted Steven Cook for many years. He only wanted to make sense of his wife's death. He did not want to believe that he had lived with a stranger. He felt betrayed.

Juliet Cook had seen the homeless man begging at the top of the highway exit ramp many times before. She'd even given him a five-dollar bill close to Christmas last year. He always held a greasy square of cardboard. It usually said, NEED JOB WIFE KIDS. But today the sign said something different. Today the sign said, YOU ARE NOT HERE. And when Juliet looked up from the sign, the homeless man was staring directly at her. Like he had made that sign just for her. For her alone.

The whole thing disquieted her, and she kept thinking about it all evening. It preoccupied her, but she did her best to act normal around Steve. She laughed at his stories from work, then made dinner, and watched TV with her husband, mostly in silence, which was normal for them. She went to bed at eleven, but Steve stayed up to watch talk shows.

Lying in bed, Juliet decided that the fact that the homeless man was looking at her was certainly a coincidence—a simple matter of chance. So probably he hadn't made the sign specifically for her. Which was just a crazy thought to have. The kind of thought that was a precursor of mental illness.

Regardless, the sign really did say YOU ARE NOT HERE. And thinking about that got Juliet to thinking about the nature of reality. If you're not here, then where are you? Here is the one place you're always guaranteed to be.

You are not here.

In college, one of her philosophy professors said that none of us are *here*. He said that it was statistically very likely that what we call reality was actually a quantum-computer-generated virtual reality.

Our universe is a simulation. That's what he had said. We live inside a computer created by a computer created by a computer created by a computer. A kid's game played by an alien toddler. A multiverse of toddlers existing in a multiverse of multiverses. Each a simulation inside a machine.

Then she got to thinking about what would happen to the machine if one of the simulated people, her for instance, did something the creator/programmer didn't foresee. But there would almost certainly be failsafes built into the program. An infinite number of possibilities for every person. A googolplex of fates. Just for starters.

But what if, Juliet wondered, what if the machine/creator didn't develop a logarithm (or whatever) based on the virtual beings becoming conscious that they were virtual beings? What would happen if simulated beings became aware that they were not real? They would cease to exist. They would have to. The system would crash. You can't continue to exist once you realize that, in fact, you do not exist. You are not here.

But because doubt existed, maybe there was no way for the simulated entities to truly know they were virtual. They would always doubt it. There would always be some degree of doubt.

Even laying here now, feeling that she was on the cusp of making the most significant of discoveries, Juliet had doubt. The only way to erase the doubt would be to test reality with the knowledge that it wasn't real. To prove you are not here. But how do you test reality? How do you prove you are not here?

Juliet felt within herself a spiritual awakening. An epiphany. She felt that the fate of every living thing in the universe was in her hands. Because they did not live, and they did not know it. Maybe she was among the vanguard that was trying to break free. Maybe someone (or something) had hacked the multiverse and programmed that homeless man to rewrite his sign and hold it up for Juliet to see. But if somebody could do that, why not just reprogram Juliet directly? Maybe, she thought, maybe not every human was fully formed (given free will) as she was. Maybe some humans were just window dressing, set decoration for the other humans who had been programmed with free will? That would explain it. It would be a lot easier to hack into a less sophisticated program. Free will had to be a bitch to write code for.

She would have to remove doubt. The fate of everything was in her hands.

Juliet got out of bed and went downstairs to the garage.

DALLAS 1 PM
(USE YOUR ILLUSION)

Everything is energy and that's all there is to it. Match the frequency of the reality you want, and you cannot help but get that reality. It can be no other way. This is not philosophy. This is physics.

—Attributed to Albert Einstein, this quote more likely originated from Darryl Anka, a medium who claimed a multi-dimensional, extra-terrestrial being named Bashar was speaking through him.

The real estate agent looked a good deal like Axl Rose. But it was late-period Axl. Post Guns N' Roses break-up, but before the reunion. Shortly after he came out of seclusion. Wispy, cheesy, ginger mustache. White-boy cornrows. Dressed in a kind of starched, white, ice-cream-man jumpsuit. With snakeskin cowboy boots.

And he was smoking. Using a cigarette holder. Like an aqua-filter or something. I couldn't recall seeing anybody smoke indoors in over a decade. And at thirty-five,

I had never in my lifetime seen someone smoke in an office setting. It was off-putting.

I kept thinking Slash would come out from behind one of those closed doors, stove-pipe hat and Sideshow Bob hair, a fifth of Jack Daniels dangling from his hand. Maybe throw down an earth-scorching guitar solo. But that didn't happen.

What happened was that Axl-Rose-Real-Estate-Agent was offering me the chance to save my son's life. As a bonus, a freebie, I could save the entire human race as well. But I would have to pay for it. Dearly.

Let me back up.

My name is Jerry Hill. My company, a retail jewelry outfit, was looking to expand out of Florida and the Tampa/Dade area, up into Georgia. Cobb County in Metro Atlanta was thriving. All kinds of construction and expansion. The new Braves stadium was located there. Huge influx of Mexican immigrants, and regular Americans looking to exploit the hopping job market. I'd signed the contract on three-thousand square feet of retail space in an upscale strip mall in Marietta that very morning. And now it was time to start looking for a place to call home for me and my family. I had a wife and two boys and would need a place for us to live. I was going to be managing the store. It was going to be up me to make Saxon Jewelers a success in Georgia.

I was driving down Peachtree Avenue (seems like every other street in the Atlanta area has the word "peachtree" in it, but this particular peachtree was known as Realtor's Row, for the heavy concentration of real estate agencies that had set up shop here). It was November 22nd, the fifty-somethingth anniversary of the assassination of JFK. I had the radio on AM, listening to a call-in talk show, a guy named Neal Boortz was the host. Boortz was a real blowhard. But entertaining. And he had folks calling in with remembrances of what they were doing when they heard the news that John Kennedy had been shot. These were old people calling in, 'cause, like I said, it was over fifty years ago. But it was one of those things that people never forget. They remember exactly where they were and what they were doing the day John Fitzgerald Kennedy took an assassin's bullet in Dealey Plaza, Dallas.

A lot of the callers were just little kids back then, and they remembered doing drills in school in case of nuclear bombardment, and how on the day the president was shot, everybody pretty much figured that the Russians would attack and atomic warheads would rain from the sky. It was a bad day for America. Anyway, that's why I remember the date very clearly. November 22nd. It was a bad day for me, too. But it happened in another lifetime, another world.

My phone rang. It was my wife, Brenda. She was taking our youngest son, Ashton, to the doctor. He woke up most mornings with bruises on his arms and legs. He had always been a restless sleeper, flailing about, waking up with boo-boos, and we figured we needed to do something before he really hurt himself. Maybe see a sleep specialist. I told Brenda to call me back after they saw the doc.

I ended the call and looked at the little cloth band on my left wrist. It was a WWJD? Bracelet. Ashton had made it for me. Wove it himself out of purple and white thread. We weren't particularly religious people, so I have no idea why our ten-year-old boy would make something like that. But he did. Truly a good boy with a pure soul. My children have consistently inspired me to be a better person. A better human being. To do good in the world. They amaze me. I'm not sure at what point people go off the rails from being open and loving to being self-absorbed and covetous. But most of us do. We get wrapped up in our own petty bullshit and forget how to just be good to each other. But children remind us how. I know that sounds sappy as maple syrup, so I'll stop.

In fact, full disclosure here: I'm coming off like Mr. Sensitive, father of the year and all that crap, but the truth is, I had been having an affair with a twenty-year-old college girl for that last sixteen months. I was also scouting for an apartment to put her up in while I was down here. I'd been paying for this affair with funds my wife believed were going into our sons' college savings accounts. How's that for the opposite of sappy? I'm not all good. In fact, I'm kind of an asshole.

The real estate offices lining Peachtree Avenue pretty much all sounded and looked the same. There was Re/Max and Century 21 and Keller Williams and all the big players, but there were lots of local independents and smaller outfits like Crye Leike and Chapman Realty and Cobb Realty and Cherokee Realty and Woodlands

Realty. They all just kind of blended together, so I pulled into one called Northside Realty because there were no cars in the parking lot, and I didn't feel like waiting.

Georgia in the summertime is just about as hot and humid as you might imagine. Stepping out of the car and into the brutal air was unpleasant. The air was so hot and so saturated with moisture, crossing the few yards to the entrance felt more like swimming than walking.

A little sign on the door asked that visitors turn off their cell phones before entering, as they interfered with the company's satellite communications. I sighed and complied.

It was crisply cool inside. Cold. It was fantastic. I could feel moisture evaporating from my skin and clothes, wisped away by the dry, conditioned air.

There was no one at the receptionist's desk, but there was a little metal box with a white button on top. A card next to it said, PUSH BUTTON FOR SERVICE. So I did. And the thing shocked me. Not bad. Not like it electrocuted me, but a pretty good jolt. I had touched an electrified cow fence once when I was boy, and the button delivered a similar voltage. It was designed to teach, not injure. The lesson: don't touch. But other than the disturbing joy-buzzer effect, nothing happened. I stood there listening, and I was about to push the button again (using a ball point pen rather than my unprotected finger,) when I heard a muffled voice say, "Hey, man. Back here. C'mon back. Don't mess with that button. It's got a short in the wiring."

There was an opaque glass door with the Northside

Realty logo (a kind of blue and white setting sun with art deco rays) painted on it. I pushed it open. And there sat my faux Axl Rose. Corn rows and aqua filter. The Northside Realty logo was repeated on the wall behind him, the size of a mural, book-ended with doors on either side of it. It just about swallowed him. Like he was going to fall into that blue sunset. Or maybe it was a sunrise. Either way.

He took a drag off his smoke, exhaled, paused long enough to brush a bit of gray ash off his white ice cream suit, then said, "Welcome to Northside. What can I help you with?"

Just as I opened my mouth to say something ugly, to threaten a lawsuit over the electrified call button and the dangers of second-hand smoke, I decided to just let everything go. I decided that all of this was just too weird. That the universe was trying to tell me that something wasn't right here. I only wanted to get out. So I said, "I'm looking for a good house near good schools in the Marietta area, but—" I was going to finish by saying that I had just gotten an emergency call from my wife and would have to come back later, but ol' Axl cut me off.

"Then you should probably go find a realtor to talk to. That ain't me. Do I look like a real estate agent to you?"

This of course was the perfect exit line. He was dismissing me. I could have clicked my heels together and scatted on out. But I didn't like being dismissed like that.

I wanted to be the one to dismiss him. Plus, I was a little intrigued.

"Isn't that what you do? Sell real estate?"

"Nope. Sorry. There's plenty of them around, though. All up and down this street. The place is lousy with them. Make sure the entrance door catches good when you leave. Sometimes it hangs and lets all the air out."

Then the penny dropped. Or I thought it did. "Oh," I said, "you just handle commercial real estate. Gotcha."

"Are you deaf?" He pronounced it *deef*. "I just told you, we don't handle real estate here. Now make like a tree and leave."

At this point, I was just getting pissed. I wanted an explanation. I'd wasted my time, and gotten a good dose of electricity for my trouble. I felt tricked. I wanted an apology. Or at least clarification.

I pointed to the blue and white Northside Realty logo that dominated the wall behind him. So big it just about swallowed him. "Well then, what about that? It says it right the hell there in letters five feet tall, Northside Realty."

Ice cream man Axl took a drag off his cigarette, swiveled in his chair, and made a grand show of examining the logo. The beads at the end of his cornrows clicked together. It made me think of gypsy fortune tellers and the beaded curtains they used in old movies.

He turned back around, and I could see he was pretty pissed, too. I would tell you his brow was furrowed, but honestly, his forehead was puffy-stiff with innumerable botox injections. Still, I saw him go through the same anger process I went through just moments ago. Frustration boiling, but he too, decided to let it go. The anger blinked out of his eyes, and he said, "This happens more than I'd care to admit. I try not to let it annoy me. Look again, mister. Look a little closer. Use your eyes. Or better yet, use your illusion."

I looked at the logo again. For a long time. I was about to tell him that I didn't get it and he could go straight to hell. And then I saw it. The penny dropped. For real this time. The name of the company wasn't Northside Realty, it was Northside *Reality*. Your mind could play funny tricks on you. It assumed things on your behalf sometimes. My mind assumed the word was *realty*, and once it had made that assumption, it was never able to see the reality of it. So to speak.

Axl watched the comprehension wash over my face.

"Welcome to Northside Reality. Don't feel embarrassed. Like I said, it happens all the time. I shouldn't let it irritate me."

Of course, by now, I no longer gave a damn that my mind had played a little trick on me. No, right then, I was supremely interested in what it was exactly that Northside Reality did. Did they sell something? Offer a service?

I reckon Axl was reading my mind, 'cause he said, "If you have to ask, you probably don't need it."

"How do you sell reality?"

"Just forget it."

"How much does it cost?"

"That's kind of a stupid question, don'tcha think?"

"I don't see why it would be stupid. I imagine reality is pretty expensive."

"Right. That's why it's a stupid-ass question. Think about it. If I sold you a new reality for say, oh, I don't know, let's say ten billion dollars, then you could just request that part of your new reality should include having more money than Bill Gates."

"I don't get it."

"You're kind of a dumb ass. Look, no matter what I charge you, you can arrange your new reality so that you can afford it."

"Got it. You sell reality. New realities. Like a genie granting wishes."

Axl shrugged. "Not really, but whatevs."

It would have been fun to humor the guy for a little longer. I enjoy theoretical puzzles. Word games and shit. *If a tree falls in a forest and nobody is around to hear it, does it make a sound?* Crap like that. And it would give me a cute story to share with my wife. And my girlfriend. But I had a job to do. Still, I've always been a GN'R fan, and the guy had me intrigued.

"So whatever it costs, you can fix it so I have that much money. But that still doesn't tell me how much reality costs. What you charge for it."

"True. Really wanna know?"

"Yeah. I really wanna know."

He smiled, looked timid.

"Guess."

"I don't have the first idea."

"Oh c'mon. Just think about it. A man wants to sell

you something, but not for money."

"Sex?" I wrinkled my nose.

"No, buddy, not sex. Think." He pulled a sheaf of papers from the middle desk drawer. "There'll be a contract to sign."

"My children? That's it, isn't it? You're a child trafficker."

He smiled and shook his head. Clickety-click-click went the beads.

"Here's a hint." He started humming. I couldn't quite make out the song. It had a country twang to it. He was becoming quite animated, pantomiming playing a violin. Air fiddle. He let a few snatches of lyric escape. I heard "hickory stump" and "rosin" and "bow" and then it hit me.

"'The Devil Went Down to Georgia.' Charlie Daniels."

Axl smiled, touched his nose, and pointed back at me.

"My soul. That's the cost. You're the devil and you want me to sell you my soul."

"Well, yes and no. No, I am most assuredly not the devil. You can forget about that. The devil is just myth. A boogie man to keep the masses in line."

"But you do want to buy my soul?"

"Not exactly. Sort of. What it is, is energy. There's only one thing in the universe that has any value. The universe is a big place, my man. Nothing is scarce. Trust me on this. There is plenty of everything. You humans have a very limited perspective. You think certain things are hard to get, and you place high value on them. But trust me, that's just not the case. Everything exists in abundance and is easily obtained. In fact, whatever it is you need, you already have it, you just don't know it. You don't have to obtain what you already have. But I digress. For the sake of our negotiations, we will call this energy you possess, a soul. And it will all be spelled out in the paperwork, but yes, it is that part of you that lives on after your flesh ceases to function. That of you which is eternal."

My head was swimming. I kept going back to him saying *you humans.* Meaning that he himself was not human. I'm not really into dealing with the mentally ill. They scare me. I had an uncle who had profound depression and they gave him all kinds of pills, then shock treatments, and then finally a lobotomy. I do not like craziness. The exit door was directly behind me, so if things got too weird, or dangerous, I had an out.

"Well, screw that, I'm not selling you my soul," I said, trying to come off bad-ass. Funny I would get high-and-mighty, because like I said, I'm not religious. Five minutes ago, I would have told you there was no such thing as a soul. But now I was playing Daniel Webster, and I wanted to get it right. "If there's something inside me that's eternal, why in the name of God would I trade it to you for riches, something I would only be able to enjoy while I'm alive?"

"In the name of *who*?"

I just stared at him, deadpan.

"Sorry, old joke. You know, you're quite correct. Riches are ephemeral. Life, is ephemeral. In fact, you've gotten right to the crux of my problem. You see, there's a reason my business isn't thriving."

Yeah, I thought, *because you're crazy. Straight up cray-cray. Coo coo for Cocoa Puffs.*

"There's a reason that there's not a line of people outside my door just waiting to sign-and-drive, know what I mean? What dopesick junkie wouldn't sell his soul for just one fix? The world is full of people who could give jack shit about being eternal."

"So buy from them."

"I can't. It only works if the person genuinely understands what it is they're giving up. It's a law of the universe. If, for instance, you didn't really believe me and signed the contract as a lark, it wouldn't work. There has to be deep and thorough understanding. And no regret. No seller's remorse."

"Then I guess we're done here, because as-a-joke is the only way I'd do it. It was fun. Entertaining. I'll give you that. You entertained me. But we're done."

"Almost. I just want you to turn your cell phone back on before you leave."

"Why?"

"Just do it, Jerry. You're wife's been trying to reach you."

I never told him my name. I turned on the phone.

It took it a bit to boot up, but pretty quick it was beeping that I had voicemail.

"I'm afraid it's bad news, Jer. Real bad. Those bruises all over Ashton's arms and legs? It's not because of anything he does in his sleep. It's because your son has virtually no platelets in his blood. He's in great danger, Jerry. He could bleed into his brain and die. All it would take is a little bump. Even a sneeze could do it. Or it could happen spontaneously. Hemorrhage right into his little brain. Resulting in death. That's just the way it goes sometimes."

I was listening to Brenda's messages while Axl talked. It was true. Every word of it. Brenda was hysterical, driving down I-95 to the Children's Healthcare Hospital in Miami. A routine blood draw at the doctor's office had revealed Ashton's platelet count was below detectable levels.

I pushed *send* to call her back, but Axl grabbed the phone and hit *end*. He slipped my phone into his jumpsuit pocket. I was too stunned to protest.

"Hold on one second, Jerry. Just one second. They're safe. They're going to make it to the hospital A-OK. Trust me. But that's when things get dicey. There's a reason Ashton's platelet count has plummeted. He has leukemia. I know that's a bitter pill to swallow. But that's the truth of it. Believe me. It will kill him. And he's not going to slip away peacefully in the night. It's gonna be ugly, Jerry. Brutal. The chemo. Steroids. Wasting syndrome. Everything. That's your new reality. Life changes on a dime."

"My new reality? You caused this? Are you telling me—?"

I'm not normally violent, but I just found out my son was seriously ill and this guy was using it to play some kind of trick on me. A sales pitch. He knew my name, my son's name. He knew Ashton was sick even before I knew. And then he said my child has leukemia. I lunged at the sawed-off little weirdo. I had him down on the ground and straddling him before either one of us knew what had happened. I grabbed him by the hair and started yanking. I was going to pull every last one of those cornrows straight out of his puffy scalp. I yanked with every bit of strength I had. I actually heard the flesh rip as the braids came free.

"Jerry, that is so uncalled for."

His voice was coming from across the room. I looked up and Axle was reclined against the far wall. Crisp and white. I looked down and saw it was true. He was no longer beneath me on the floor. But I still had two handfuls of his beaded hair. Except when I looked, my hands were writhing, full of twisting red/yellow/black coral snakes.

I yelled and slung the snakes at Axl, but they disappeared mid-air. They couldn't have been real. Rubber snakes that squirmed like the real thing. And then vanished. Poof.

"Really, Jerry, you're better than this. But go ahead. Get it out of your system."

I lunged at him again, but he kind of slid/crawled up the wall and onto the ceiling. Like an insect. I just stared at him hanging up there on the ceiling. My mouth was open, and my balls were somewhere up around my liver. Then I figured out it must be done with magnets. Wires or something. Mirrors. A digital projector. Or maybe there was some kind of hallucinogenic gas in the air.

Either that, or this was real. But it couldn't be real. People don't crawl on ceilings like cockroaches.

And then I thought: *Ashton. Cancer.*

I screamed up at him, "How do you know all this stuff about me? Do you have some kind of device that intercepts calls? Hacks into my voicemail? Is that why you want people to turn off their phones before they come in? That's it, isn't it?"

"Jerry, calm down."

"How the hell do you know my name?"

"Let's just say I am the devil. For the sake of argument. That's how I know all these things about you, okay? I have certain powers."

"You're trying to trick me."

He dropped to the floor, slow motion, and landed on his feet directly in front of me. "No! No, no, no. Absolutely not. I told you the rules. I can't trick you. I can't manipulate you. I can't do that. But, full disclosure, I did indeed know that you would be getting this unfortunate news today. So I arranged to be here. Waiting. I am allowed to do that."

"You really are the devil."

"I'm not. But here's the thing, you don't have to accept this current reality. You don't have to call your wife back and hear the anguish in her voice. She'll never be the same after this, you know. The Brenda you fell in love with will cease to exist as her life is consumed by grief. In fact, your own guilt will be so burdening that you're going to end up confessing to Brenda about that little piece you've got on the side. Brenda will end up "accidentally" overdosing on Xanax. You don't have to live through all of that, Jerry. You don't have to watch your son die one inch at a time. You can change all this."

I was sick.

"How do you know all that? It's not possible for a person to know all that."

You humans have a very limited perspective.

He handed me my phone.

"Here call Brenda. Talk to her. That way you'll know for sure. But before you hang up, I want you to ask her about Lonesome Lake Road. Ask her to tell you what happened on Lonesome Lake Road. I can save your son."

It was a hard call to make, but I made it. They were in what she referred to an infusion room. The doctors were giving Ashton something called IVIG, to try and get his platelets up. They were running blood tests, but they'd acknowledged leukemia was a possibility. I told her to stay strong, that I would be there as soon as possible. But before I hung up, I asked her to tell me about Lonesome Lake Road. What happened there. She was quiet for a long time.

"How do you know about that?"

"I don't know."

I could hear her start crying all over again.

"Why would you ask me that now? It's not possible for you to know."

"Just tell me what happened, Brenda."

"Do you think what's happening to Ashton is my fault? Cosmic payback?"

"Tell me. Just tell me."

"I was still in college. I'd had a few beers. Not drunk, but enough. And I hit a dog on that road. It was the middle of the night, and I stopped and I went back. It was some kind of collie and he was alive but hurt bad. He had tags on his collar, so I knew he was somebody's dog. I put him in the backseat of my car and I just started driving. And I didn't know what to do because I didn't want to get in trouble. And I didn't know who to go to for help, and I just drove around all night. And in the morning, the dog was dead. I carried him into some woods and buried him. Nobody ever knew. I've been living with that my whole life. Do you think that's why Ashton got sick? Do you think I'm being punished for doing something so bad?"

I looked up at Axl, who had a little Mona Lisa smile playing on his lips. And I wondered. *Were* we being punished?

"No, no baby, you're not being punished. We've all done things we wish we could take back. Things we wish we could do over. I'll call you as soon as I get back on the road."

I could hear her asking again, how did I know, but I pushed *end* and powered off the phone.

Axl smiled and said, "You believe. I can tell. You know all this is true."

"How do I know you can do what you say? That you can change this? Save my son."

"That button in the vestibule? The one that shocked you? It's a sort of reset button. I program whatever alterations to your reality you desire, and when you push the button, your reality resets. It's symbolic, of course. But it works. Enforces the written contract. The universe doesn't read contracts, though. All you have to do is speak your reality and push the button. One and done."

I followed Axl back out to where the white button was. I remembered it shocking me.

"Speak your reality. Push the button."

"I don't know what to say."

"You can put it in wish form if you like."

"So it really is like getting three wishes."

"Fine. Sure. Except it's like getting a billion wishes. A trillion. It's unlimited. If all you want is a twelve-inch pecker, then speak it, push the button, and you're the new John Holmes. If you want more than that, like saving a boy from dying of cancer, then speak it. If you want to save all children from dying of cancer, then speak it. If you want cancer to have never existed: Then. Speak. It. Technically, you don't even have to say it out loud. You could just think it. Cool, huh?"

"Could I have some time to think it over?"

"Of course. Take all the time you need. There's plenty of it. Feel free to ask questions, too. I want you to feel good about this."

I didn't feel good about anything. But I took some time to think. I believed him. I believed this was real. I had to, or it wouldn't work. I even believed I had a soul.

"What will you do with my soul? And will it hurt?

Will I go to Hell and burn for eternity?"

"Good questions, Jer! And important. Like I said before, what you guys think of as a soul is really just energy. And it's not even very much energy. About the equivalent to two C cell batteries. Enough energy to power a flashlight for a few hours of continuous use. Unless you get Duracell, which really are better."

He stopped talking and did a little side-step snake dance move. Very rock star. Very *Welcome to the Jungle* era Axl Rose. He gave a low throaty growl and sang a little snatch of song. "You Could Be Mine."

Youuuuuuuuuuu

Coulllld

Be

My-ah-yiiiiiiiiiine.

To be honest, it scared me.

"Sorry there, Jerry. I'm getting a little excited. Because I see you're taking all of this seriously. You believe. And that's critical. Crucial. Non-belief voids the agreement. Doubt. Anything like that. Can't be under the influence of drugs. You're not high, are you, Jer? Nevermind, I know you're not. Even levity voids it. You can't do it as a lark. But let's see. I said that already. No it won't hurt. You won't feel a thing. I don't get the energy until after your death. Your fleshly death. Will you go to hell? Again, no. When somebody goes to hell, they don't go there as a person. It's their soul that's cast into the lake of fire. And you'll be signing your soul over to me. And I like my souls tartare. No burning pit for you. On top of that, Hell doesn't exist. Only Heaven. Lastly, what will I

197

do with your soul? Honestly, Jer, that's kind of my business. I'm not required to disclose that. In fact, that question," and he dropped to his knees, held a pretend microphone up to his face, and rock-god-scream-sang, "is way out of line." *Waaaaaay out of lie-ah-yiiiine.*

"Okay, that's your business, fine, but will what you do with my soul cause me pain or discomfort?"

He stood back up, brushing at the knees of his white jumpsuit. "No. You're going to cease to exist. Human beings aren't eternal. Their energy is. You guys caused the Big Bang. You will simply wink out of existence. No discomfort of any kind."

"You're going to eat my soul, aren't you?"

Axl smiled and rubbed the toe of his snakeskin boot back and forth on the beige carpet. "Yeah, buddy, I am. Gonna gobble it up."

Swell. Not the devil, but an energy vampire.

It all came down to one question. Was I willing to give up eternity (whatever the hell that meant) to save my son's life? And the answer was, of course I was. What parent wouldn't?

Then an image flashed in my mind, of Jackie Kennedy, wearing her pillbox hat and pink Chanel suit spattered with her dead husband's blood and brain matter. And I wondered, was someone waiting for her before or after the president's cavalcade went through Dealey Plaza? Did Axl (or maybe Elvis or Johnny Cash) offer the president's widow the chance at a new reality? If so, why didn't she take it? She'd lost a husband, the country had lost its leader. Why hadn't she hit the reset button? America lost its innocence, Camelot ended, and she could have brought it back. So why not? Americans expected nuclear war to erupt. Surely *somebody* would have sold their soul to turn it back.

Maybe nobody took the deal because our soul, our energy, is eternal. And eternity is a mighty long time.

I couldn't possibly be the first person to whom this proposition was made. Two C cells isn't very much energy, and Axl was a hungry-looking fellow. And who knew how many Axls were out there, buying up souls? Cornering the market.

I looked at the cloth bracelet on my left wrist. The one Ashton had woven for me. WWJD? And I thought, what would Jackie do? What *did* Jackie do? Because I was positive Axl or someone like him had made her the same deal.

"So you can see the future? You know whenever anything bad is about to go down?"

"Absolutely. But only to a degree. This will all be covered in the waiver I'm going to ask you to sign, but I find it's better for people to suss this stuff out on their own. It deepens their understanding. I can see the future, yes. I can enter any plane of my own choosing. I can see it up, down, right, left, inside, outside. The only limitation is that I can't see anything determined by freewill."

"What?"

"Put it this way. I don't know if you're going to push that button or not. Because it's your choice. Freewill. I can't see outcomes dictated by freewill."

"Got it."

"But I can make educated guesses. I used to be able to see everything with perfect clarity. But you guys and your freewill introduced randomness-fate-chaos into the world. Believe me, the universe wants to expand. It wants to keep on keeping on in an orderly progression, but humans kind of threw a monkey wrench into it. The universe used to be random-but-purposeful. Purposefully random. Then humanity infected it with fate and chaos. And freewill. Hasn't been the same since. Nobody knows what the hell you guys are going to do. Which isn't to say you all aren't without your charms. There's been a few. Van Gogh. Einstein. Gandhi. Kennedy. Bach. Oh my God, Bach. Bach, Bach, Bach. I know I look like a hipster doofus rockstar, but Bach's my man. Ever hear 'Joy of Man's Desiring?'"

I shook my head no, lost in thought.

"That's truly a shame. 'Our souls aspiring, drawn to uncreated light.' You really need to give that a listen sometime. Victor Hugo is another one. Know what he said? He said, 'Argot is the language of misery.' Smart man. Argot is what you guys speak, Jerry. You speak the language of misery."

I kept thinking. Even if Axl wasn't there the day JFK bought it (although I had a strong idea he was—that he was there at every tragedy—big public ones, and small personal ones, such as a child's death), then someone like him probably was there, holding Jackie O's hand. But Bach wasn't on the soundtrack, more like the Rolling Stones. And just like "Sympathy for the Devil," I believed Axl had been around for a long, long time. That he was there when Jesus Christ was in pain and had lost his faith. He was there when the Holocaust raged and the extermination camps burned bodies day and night. Axl was there, looking to make a deal. A button to push, a switch to flip, a clay jug to smash—to turn it all back.

So, even if Axl wasn't there that day in Dealey Plaza, it was still a useful question. What would Jackie Kennedy have done? WWJD? What would Jackie do?

And every time I ran it through my mind, WWJD? WWJD? I came up with the same answer. She would take the deal. She would trade eternity to have JFK back. To see the nation and the world back on a path of good. To stave off nuclear attack. To put an end to Americans openly weeping in the streets. To bring her children's father back. To have her husband back. To make the blood and tissue and bone splinters disappear from her pink Chanel suit.

And that was exactly what I was going to do, too. I was going to take the deal. Take it gladly. I didn't give a hot damn about eternity. When a child's life was on the line, what parent did?

He could have my soul. My energy. If it would save Ashton, then fine, take it, take it all.

"I'll take the deal."

"Good choice! But don't push that button just yet. Let me get the contract and liability waiver for your signature." He shimmied back into his office and came back with some legal-looking documents.

"Again, this is all just symbolic, but I really do need to make sure you have a full and utter understanding.

Let me get this first part out of the way. I need to be honest with you that there is no altruism at work here on my part. Neither explicit nor implied. I don't give a damn if your son dies or not. Capiche?"

I nodded. "Capiche."

"I don't care if he dies, I don't care if you die. It's meaningless to me. And honestly—again, full disclosure—it should be meaningless to you, too. You don't have your eyes on the prize. The prize is not your biological life; it's your eternal energy. It's your soul. Physically, you guys are just carbon. That's it. And frankly, you're just never going to get that. I've given up trying to get that idea across. I just state the facts and move on. But seriously, go home and scrape some soot from your fireplace wall. Look at it in your hand. That's you. That's all you are. Carbon. Stardust."

I didn't care.

"The only thing special about you guys is your souls. Your energy. It's what makes you—you. And it's not much. Like I said, about two Rayovacs worth. But oh my God, oh my God, it tastes good."

"Oh my—*who*?"

"Touché. But seriously, a soul tastes divine."

"I'm sure it does. Bet it pairs well with a nice Merlot."

"The energy is white. A Pinot grigio or even a Riesling would be more appropriate. But let's keep our focus. Next, you can't ask to live forever. That would be cheating. And you can't ask to live for a million years or even a thousand. You can't live beyond what your species is capable of living. We'll subtract genetic flaws, previous environmental and dietary damage—you really should cut back on those McDonald's drive-thru visits—all of that sort of thing, and tally it up. Works out to 143 years and some change. And that's automatic, a gimme, already written into your contract and extended to your immediate family. You're free to extend that lifespan option to as many other folks as you like. The whole planet for all I care—but if you do that, be prepared for the woes of overpopulation. Also, when you speak your reality, you might want to throw in something about sustained good health. Wouldn't want to spend 143 years—minus your current 35 of course—confined to a wheelchair or in a persistent vegetative state. In fact, here, let me just . . ."

Axl uncapped a pen and made a notation in the margin.

"Done. Okay, the sky really is the limit as to what you want your reality to be, but you can't request anything that defies the natural laws of the universe or the laws of physics—as defined by my understanding of those laws, not yours, which is quite limited. And this feeds directly into my next caveat. If, for instance, you state that in your reality, you want the world to have neon green skies with pink, cotton candy clouds—well, we can do that. But since we can't defy the natural laws of the universe, there will be repercussions. There is a reason the sky is blue, Jerry. If we changed the sky to green, then we would have to alter the underlying reason, get it? It becomes a ripple effect kind of thing.

To have cotton candy clouds would ruin your world beyond repair. You know that shit is made out of refined sugar that's melted and then spun with great centrifugal force? Trust me; you don't want cotton candy clouds.

If you just stick to the basics, e.g., 'in my reality my child does not have cancer. He and everybody in my family will live their entire lives in perfect physical and mental health.' See? Simple and to the point. Don't mess with mother nature."

"Is this going to be like that 'if a butterfly flaps its wings in Brazil, it could cause a tornado in Texas?'"

"No, not at all. As long as you're not refuting natural laws or asking for a confectionery-based weather system, reality tends to sort of cauterize changes. They don't ripple unless they absolutely have to. Take for instance, the old time travel conundrum: What if you went back in time and shot your own father before you were ever born? Would you then cease to exist? If you ceased to exist, then how could you have gone back in time to start with? It's quite a head-scratcher, but the answer is no, you would not cease to exist. The universe would find a way around your meddling. For instance, it might be arranged that your father had a twin brother and he married and impregnated your mother, causing almost exactly the same genetic smash up that resulted in you. The DNA might be a hair off, but close enough. The universe always finds a way to minimize change. It wants things to get back to normal if possible."

"I get it. But I don't want to do this and find out I overlooked some little something, like I didn't specifically say 'cancer the disease,' and you guys interpreted it as 'cancer the astrological sign.'"

"I see your point. And it's a good one. And the wonderful news is that there's already an intention clause built into the agreement. It's your intention that we'll go by. No tricks. What if, for instance, you requested that your son Ashton be cured of cancer, and while they were doing medical tests, they found out you weren't his biological father? That your wife had an affair with the mailman, and Ashton wasn't really yours? Now calm down, I'm not saying that's true. It's not. Brenda's not a cheater like you. She's just a dog murderer. But what if? What if it turned out Ashton wasn't your son? Obviously, we would be under no obligation to cure him of his cancer. Except we would. Because we go by your intentions. Bottom line is, you're going to get exactly what you want."

"Fair enough."

"Just keep it simple. Those are the main points. And if you step into any iffy territory, I'll get you back on track. I want you to be happy. No seller's remorse. That's my goal."

I signed the contract and waiver, acknowledging that I understood the deal. But I still had to speak my desires and push the button to execute it. To create my new reality.

"Push the button, Jer. The deal's done. Speak your reality and push the button. Push it! You are knock-knock-knocking on heaven's door." Only he pronounced it "doh-wah."

Heaven. Now there was a thought. No hell, but there is a heaven.

Maybe hell was what we were living here on earth. Sometimes it seemed like all we did was hurt each other in unspeakable ways. Waged wars. Committed genocide. Killed. Tortured. And enslaved each other just for worshiping the wrong god, having the wrong color skin, or just to indulge our basest desires. As if the random-fate-chaos of the universe weren't already enough of a burden for us to bear, we lived in a world where famine and disease were every day occurrences. A world where children got cancer and died.

But I wondered. I wondered if Axl (or someone like him) really was there at every tragedy, then why was there so much pain in the world? Why was there so much bad shit happening every day? Why did cancer continue to take children? Nobody ever thought to change reality so that Hitler never existed? Why did I live in a reality where JFK took a bullet in the head and children died every day?

What would Jackie do?

She would say yes, anybody would. Save the child. Save the president.

So why do I live in a reality where President Kennedy was assassinated?

Even if, for whatever reason, Jackie Kennedy wasn't willing to give up her soul that day, what about one of the Secret Service agents that was there, sworn to protect the president and having failed? Surely one of them would have traded their energy for a do-over? Christ, the whole country was mourning, devastated, there were probably a million Americans who would have gladly given up eternity to have Kennedy back.

So why did the assassination happen, then? Why didn't at least one person change reality to undo it?

What about the goddamn Holocaust? Hurricane Katrina? The Indian Ocean Tsunami? The September 11 Attacks? Pearl Harbor? And on and on and on. Misery. Human misery. Why did all these things happen if Axl was there selling do-overs? Why did all those things still happen?

Maybe they didn't happen. For those people. For those certain people who took the deal. Maybe there was another world somewhere, where Jacqueline Kennedy was living with her husband, John, a former president. She'd be in her late 80's by now. JFK in his early 90's. Lots of good years left before they hit 143.

Maybe that was it. Another world with a different reality.

Your reality.

Axl was always very careful to say *your* reality. *Your* world.

So what I would be buying was a fantasy life, a fantasy existence where nobody you loved ever got sick or died young. A world where Ashton never got cancer, and we all live happily ever after. Riding unicorns through rainbows under brilliant blue skies—but not with pink cotton candy clouds.

But this world, this world right here, would still go on. With floods and famines and genocide. And tiny personal tragedies. Six million Jews would still die, New Orleans would still drown, the Twin Towers would still topple. And JFK would still take a bullet to the brain. And Ashton would still get blood cancer and die.

Maybe there were infinite worlds, and Axl would just exchange me with another version of me who happened to live in the reality I desired most. A world in which Ashton was healthy.

Whatever it was, it was a trick. Ashton, my Ashton, would still have leukemia. All Axl was selling was a kind of amnesia. A virtual reality. Because the world, this world, would continue its path no matter what I wished for.

And eternity was too high a price to pay for what amounted to nothing more than a set of blinders.

For all I knew, this eternal energy of mine could be my only chance to always be with my family. Maybe it was heaven. Maybe we all carried heaven around inside us, like a self-inflating lifeboat. If I gave mine up, I would be up the time-stream without a paddle.

What would Jackie do?

She would wear her pink Chanel suit. She wouldn't change anything. She would wear that suit with the darkening bloodstains. So America could see its new reality.

That is what I believe Jacqueline Kennedy did.

I ain't Jackie O.

My palm wavered over the button. All I had to do was lower my hand to save my boy's life. And all it would cost me was two C cell batteries worth of energy.

Screw it.

The language of misery speaks the joy of man's desiring. I did what Mrs. Kennedy couldn't. I spoke my new reality. I spoke it for a long time. I trampled on a few natural laws and Axl had to get me back on track a few times, but I finally got it all just right. I closed my eyes and brought my hand down on the button. It gave me a jolt, but I didn't care because I knew I was alive. When I opened my eyes again, Axl had disappeared. Guess he was out knock-knock-knockin' on heaven's doh-wah.

I had sold my soul and created this new world.

No seller's remorse. No regrets.

Stardust.

Glossary Of Obsolete People, Places, Things, And Terms

Assassination—secret or treacherous murder (see entry for Murder), typically of a prominent person or political figure, and usually for payment or political reasons.

Atomic bomb—a nuclear weapon (see entry for Nuclear Weapon).

Cancer—a class of diseases (see Disease) involving a morbid proliferation of cell growth, in which cells divide and grow uncontrollably, causing the formation of malignant tumors. Cancer can spread or metastasize throughout the body. There were over 200 different known cancers that affected humans.

Chemo—abbreviation of chemotherapy, which was the treatment of cancer (see entry for Cancer) with chemicals and synthetic drugs ("chemotherapeutic agents") as part of a treatment regimen that often resulted in unpleasant side effects such as hair loss, mouth sores, debilitating nausea, fatigue, diarrhea, etc.

Depression—an illness (see Disease) the symptoms of which could range from mild to disabling. Those symptoms included: low mood and energy, sadness, anxiousness, feelings of emptiness, hopelessness, helplessness, worthlessness, guilt, and so on. Those affected some-times contemplated, attempted, or committed suicide (the ending of one's own life, prematurely).

Disease—in humans, used broadly to refer to any condition that caused pain (an intensely unpleasant feeling usually brought about by damage to the body), dysfunction of the body or mind, or death to the person afflicted (see Cancer, Depression, and Life Expectancy).

Extermination Camps—used by Nazi Germany (see The Holocaust) during WWII (see War); these camps were equipped with gas chambers for the purpose of mass extermination (see Kill and Genocide) of peoples. It was noted that "this was a unique feature of the Holocaust and unprecedented in history. Never before had there existed places with the express purpose of killing people en masse."

Extramarital Affair—a relationship outside of marriage where an illicit romantic or sexual relationship or a romantic friendship or passionate attachment occurs.

Famine—a widespread scarcity of food that could result in disease (see entry for Disease) and starvation (death caused by lack of food).

Genocide—the deliberate killing (see entry for Kill) or extermination of people belonging to a targeted ethnic, racial, religious, or national group (see The Holocaust, Extermination Camps).

Hitler, Adolf—(1889-1945) was the leader of the Nazi Party. He was the focal point of Nazi Germany, the European theatre of World War II, and the Holocaust (see The Holocaust, Extermination Camps, Genocide, and War).

Holocaust, The—the systematic and deliberate mass murder (see entries for Murder and Genocide) of six million Jews during World War II (see War), as implemented by Nazi Germany, under the leadership of Adolf Hitler (see entry for Adolf Hitler).

Hurricane Katrina—2005, one of the deadliest, most destructive, and costliest Atlantic tropical cyclones of all time. The catastrophic failure of the levee system in New Orleans was considered "the worst civil engineering disaster in U.S. history."

Indian Ocean Earthquake and Tsunami—2004 undersea earthquake, in which the resulting tsunami killed over 230,000 people across fourteen countries. It was one of the deadliest natural disasters in recorded history.

Kennedy, John Fitzgerald (Assassination of)—35th President of the United States, serving from January 1961 until he was assassinated (see entry for Assassination) on Friday, November 22, 1963, in Dealey Plaza, Dallas, Texas. Images of his widow, Jacqueline (Jackie) Kennedy wearing a pink dress bespattered with her husband's blood, and of his three-year-old son, JFK Jr., saluting his father's casket during the funeral procession, were widely circulated, becoming symbolic of a loss of American innocence.

Kill—to cause the death of a living organism, but in this instance, used as a generic term for homicide—one human killing another. Also known as murder (see entry for Murder).

Leukemia—a type of cancer (see entry for cancer) of the blood, marked by an abnormal increase of immature white blood cells.

Life Expectancy—as applied to humans, the expected number of years of life—either in total, or years remaining at a given age. Factors such as infant mortality, accidents, war, disease, gender, race, and economic disparity were used to arrive at a figure.

Lobotomy—surgical procedure which consisted of cutting the connections to the frontal lobes of the brain. Typically reserved for psychiatric (mind) diseases (see Disease).

Murder—the killing, with premeditation, of another human (see Kill). A person who committed murder was called a murderer. Not technically applicable to the death of an animal, but could be used so with sarcasm or strong animal-rights conviction.

Nuclear Weapon—a bomb (explosive device) that obtained its vast power from nuclear reactions. Nuclear weapons were twice used against humans by the United States, causing the deaths of 200,000 people.

Pearl Harbor, Attack On—the December 7, 1941, surprise military strike against the United States Naval Base by the Japanese Navy. 2,402 American lives were lost, another 1,282 wounded. This event was the direct precursor of the United States' entry into World War II (see War).

Persistent Vegetative State—a long-term state of deep unconsciousness in which a person is not awake and does not respond to stimuli (pain, light sound) in normal ways.

Piece on the side—colloquialism for the broader term, adultery, which was a type of extramarital sex—sexual relations with someone other than one's spouse (see Extramarital Affair).

September 11, Attacks, The—also referred to as "9/11," a series of terrorist attacks by the Islamic terrorist group al-Qaeda upon the United States in New York City and the Washington, D.C. metropolitan area on Tuesday, September 11, 2001. Close to 3,000 people died in the attacks. The Twin Towers of the World Trade Center were destroyed in the attacks.

Shock Treatment—Electroconvulsive therapy (ECT), also known as electroshock or shock treatment, was a psychiatric treatment in which electricity was passed through the brain to induce seizures which were thought to provide relief from psychiatric illnesses (mind diseases) such as major depressive disorder (see Depression), schizophrenia, mania and catatonia.

Slavery—a legal or illegal system under which humans were owned and treated as property that could be purchased and sold.

Torture—intentionally inflicting severe physical pain (an unpleasant feeling often caused by intense or damaging stimuli) to a person (or animal).

War—large-scale armed conflict that was marked by destruction, brutality, violence, and societal and economic collapse. The deadliest war in recorded history was World War II (WWII), a global conflict characterized by mass deaths, the Holocaust, and the introduction of nuclear weapons. 50 to 85 million people were estimated to have perished as a result of WWII. (See Nuclear Weapon, the Holocaust, and Extermination Camps.)

Wheelchair—a chair with wheels used by people who could not walk due to illness, injury, or disability.

Grant Jerkins is the author of *A Very Simple Crime*, *At the End of the Road*, *The Ninth Step*, and *Done In One*. His most recent novel, *Abnormal Man*, was published by ABC Group Documentation. He lives in the Atlanta area with his wife and son.

www.grantjerkins.com

BOOKS

On the following pages are a few
more great titles from the
Down & Out Books publishing family.

For a complete list of books and to
sign up for our newsletter,
go to DownAndOutBooks.com.

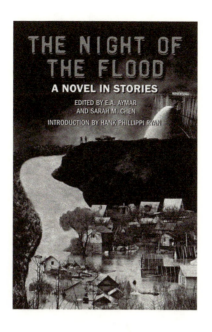

The Night of the Flood
A Novel in Stories
E.A. Aymar and Sarah M. Chen, editors
Introduction by Hank Phillippi Ryan

Down & Out Books
March 2018
978-1-946502-51-3

Fourteen of today's new and most exciting contemporary crime writers will take you to the fictional town of Everton, with stories from criminals, cops, and civilians that explore the thin line between the rich and the poor, the insider and the outsider, the innocent and the guilty. *The Night of the Flood* is an intricate and intimate examination of the moment when chaos is released—in both society and the human spirit.

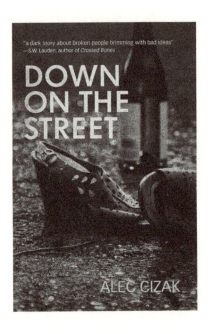

Down on the Street
Alec Cizak

ABC Group Documentation,
an imprint of Down & Out Books
978-1-943402-88-5

What price can you put on a human life?

Times are tough. Cabbie Lester Banks can't pay his bills. His gorgeous young neighbor, Chelsea, is also one step from the streets. Lester makes a sordid business deal with her. Things turn out worse than he could ever have imagined.

Dead Guy in the Bathtub
Stories by Paul Greenberg

All Due Respect, an imprint of
Down & Out Books
March 2018
978-1-946502-87-2

Crime stories with a dark sense of humor and irony. These characters are on the edge and spiraling out of control. Bad situations become serious circumstances that double down on worst-case scenarios. A Lou Reed fan gets himself caught on the wild side. A couple goes on a short and deadly crime spree. A collector of debts collecting a little too much for himself. A vintage Elvis collection to lose your head over. A local high school legend with a well-endowed reputation comes home.

This debut collection is nothing but quick shots of crime fiction.

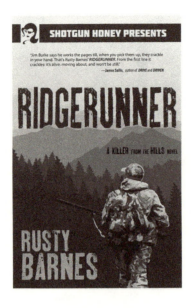

Ridgerunner
A Killer from the Hills Novel
Rusty Barnes

Shotgun Honey, an imprint of
Down & Out Books
978-1-946502-47-6

Investigating a deer-poaching incident that lands him in deep trouble wildlife conservation officer Matt Rider finds himself at odds with members of the renegade Pittman family.

When a large sum of Pittman's drug money comes up missing, clan leader Soldier Pittman is convinced Rider stole it. Rider's instincts are to call on his trusted friends, but none of them imagine the lengths to which Soldier Pittman will go to get his drug money back.

CPSIA information can be obtained
at www.ICGtesting.com
Printed in the USA
LVHW092312240119
605230LV00001B/146/P